Journey to the End of the World

To the memory of my parents

HENNING MANKELL

Journey to the End of the WORLD

Translated by Laurie Thompson

Andersen Press • London

First published in English 2008 by
Andersen Press Limited,
20 Vauxhall Bridge Road, London SWIV 2SA
www.andersenpress.co.uk

Copyright © 1998 by Henning Mankell
Original title: *Resan till världens ände*
First published by Rabén & Sjögren,
Stockholm, in 1998.
This translation © Laurie Thompson, 2008

British Library Cataloguing in Publication Data available

ISBN 978 1 84270 666 4

Mixed Sources
Product group from well-managed
forests and other controlled sources
www.fsc.org Cert no. TT-COC-0002227
© 1996 Forest Stewardship Council
FSC

Typeset by FiSH Books, Enfield, Middx.
Printed and bound in Great Britain by
CPI Bookmarque, Croydon, CR0 4TD

Foreword

This is the fourth and final book in the series about Joel.

The first part was *A Bridge to the Stars*. Then came *Shadows in the Twilight*, and *When the Snow Fell*.

In this book there are occasional references to characters who appeared in the earlier stories. I have not always bothered to describe them in detail again. What they look like, or why they do what they do.

Anybody who wants to can always check up by consulting previous volumes in the series of stories about Joel.

But it is not necessary, of course.

Most of what you need to know is to be found in these pages.

Henning Mankell

One night in March

the year when Joel would soon celebrate his fifteenth birthday, he wakes up out of a dream that has made him feel frightened. When he opens his eyes in the darkness, he doesn't know where he is at first. But then he hears his dad's snores rolling in through the half-open door.

That's the moment when his dream comes back to him.

He'd been walking over the ice on the frozen river. He didn't know why he was there. But he suddenly noticed that the ice was beginning to crack under his feet. He started running to the bank as fast as he could, but all the time more cracks opened out in front of him. He would never be able to get to the bank. Then, as if with the wave of a magic wand, all the winter ice vanished. Apart from the small floe he was standing on. Then he noticed there was something odd about the water. It wasn't black and cold like it usually was. It was boiling. And all the time the floe he was standing on was getting smaller. In the end there was nothing left of it. Fierce, white crocodiles were snapping at him. And he was falling. Falling straight into their jaws ...

When he wakes up he notices that he's covered in sweat. The hands of his alarm clock gleam in the darkness. A quarter past four. He's so relieved to have escaped from his dream. He pulls the covers up to his chin and turns to face the wall in the hope of going back to sleep. There are still a few hours to go before he needs to get up and go to school.

But he can't sleep. He lies awake. Persistent thoughts fill his mind. Three more months and his school days will come to an end. He'll get his final Report. Then what will he do? Where will he find a job? What would he really like to do? The thoughts won't go away. Especially when he thinks about Samuel. For as long as Joel can remember, his dad has been talking about moving away from the little town they live in. As soon as Joel finishes school, Samuel will become a sailor again, and take Joel with him. But the years have gone by and Samuel talks less and less about the sea. And ships. And all the ports waiting for them out there in the wide world.

There's a lot to think about. Joel sits up in bed and leans his back against the wall. It's March already. Before long the snow will start to melt away. It will be his birthday next month. He'll be fifteen. That means he'll be allowed to ride a moped. And see adults-only films. His birthday will be the day he no longer needs to sneak into the cinema without being seen. He'll be able to walk past the caretaker with a ticket in his hand.

Becoming fifteen is an important event.

But he feels worried. What will happen?

In the end he manages to go back to sleep.

Outside a solitary dog runs past the house. It's on its way to somewhere only the dog knows about.

But Joel is asleep. In his dreams the spring thaw has arrived already.

And the ice is melting ...

1

Joel was halfway down the hill just past the vicarage when his chain came off. He was so surprised that he swerved and lost control of his bike. He crashed into the hedge round the horse dealer's garden and flew headfirst into some currant bushes. One cheek was badly scratched, and his left knee was bruised. But when he scrambled to his feet he was able to stand up and rescue his bike from the hedge. He'd made a big hole in it. As the horse dealer had a fiery temper, Joel rapidly wheeled his bike away and leaned it against the vicarage fence.

It was an afternoon in the middle of May. There were still patches of snow left in the shadow of house walls and on the verges. Spring had not yet brought any warm weather with it. But every afternoon after school Joel took his bike and rode through the streets of the little town. He felt worried and restless. What was going to happen shortly? When he left school?

A few days after he'd had that dream about the river with boiling water, he'd asked Samuel. He'd prepared himself carefully. They usually had pork and fried potatoes on a Sunday, but as it was Samuel's favourite, Joel had made it for that night's dinner even though it was a Tuesday. Joel knew that the best moment to take up an important matter with Samuel was when he had just finished eating and pushed his plate to one side.

And that moment had come. Samuel put down his fork, wiped his mouth and slid his plate away.

'We have to make up our minds,' Joel said.

Although his voice had broken now, it sometimes happened that things he said came out like a squeak or in falsetto. He spoke slowly and tried to make his voice as deep as possible.

Samuel was usually tired when he'd finished eating. Now he blinked and looked at Joel.

'What do we have to make up our minds about?' he asked.

Samuel seemed to be in a good mood, Joel thought. That wasn't always the case. Samuel could sometimes be peevish, and in that case Joel knew there was hardly any point in trying to discuss something important.

'What we're going to do when I've left school.'

Samuel smiled.

'What sort of a Report are you going to get?'

Joel didn't like Samuel answering a question by asking another one himself. It was a bad habit that lots of grown-ups had.

But he had prepared himself thoroughly. Joel's school marks were always important for Samuel.

'I'll get better marks than last autumn,' he said. 'I'll be in the top three for geography.'

Samuel nodded.

'When are we going to move?' Joel asked. He must have asked Samuel that question at least a thousand times before. Nearly every day, year after year. The same question. 'When are we going to move?'

Samuel looked down at the blue tablecloth on the kitchen table. Joel thought he might as well continue.

'You're not a lumberjack,' he said. 'You're a sailor. When I've left school we won't need to stay here any longer. We can go away. We can sign on for the same ship. I'm fifteen now. I can also be a sailor.'

Joel waited for an answer.

But Samuel continued staring down at the tablecloth. Then he stood up without a word and put on the coffee water. Joel wasn't going to get an answer, that much was obvious.

He suddenly felt angry.

He'd made a big effort and prepared Sunday food even though it was only Tuesday, but still Samuel couldn't give him a sensible answer.

He thought he ought to swear and tell his father a few home truths. Tell him he had an obligation to answer now. Joel had no intention of asking the same question another thousand times.

But he didn't swear. He cleared away the plates, scraped the remains into the slop bucket and put the crockery in the sink.

'I'm going out,' he said.

'Don't you have any homework?' asked Samuel, without looking up from the coffee water that was just coming to the boil.

'I've done it already,' Joel said. 'Besides, soon there won't be any more homework.'

Joel waited. But in vain. Samuel said nothing else.

Joel took his jacket and went downstairs.

No answer this time either.

Joel thought about this the following day as well, when he was mending the chain on his bicycle. He hadn't put his question to Samuel again, but had the impression that his dad was thinking it over. Why that should be the case, Joel had no idea. But that's what he suspected, and the feeling was very strong.

It also worried him. When Samuel said hardly anything and seemed to be lost in thought, he could sometimes lapse into one of his phases. When he would just disappear, and then come home drunk late at night. It was a long time since that had happened last, but Joel knew it would happen again. Sooner or later. And that was something he always dreaded. Being forced to go out looking for Samuel, and then dragging him home when he was too drunk to walk without help.

Joel tried to wipe the oil off his bicycle chain using a sheet of newspaper that happened to be blowing past.

Let's hope it doesn't happen at the end of term ceremony, he thought. That Samuel turns up at church drunk.

Anything but that.

He turned round and gazed up at the church tower. The clock told him it was high time for him to go home and put the potatoes on to boil. He mounted his bike and started pedalling. On the gravelled area behind the petrol station, some boys were dividing into two teams. Several of them were Joel's classmates. He pedalled even harder. He always needed to make the dinner: he'd always been his own mum. And Samuel's as well, sometimes.

When he left school he'd stop doing the cooking. If Samuel wanted to eat when he came home, he'd have to prepare the food himself.

Joel kicked open the gate and freewheeled to the side of the door where he could park his bike. Then he raced up the stairs and wrenched open the kitchen door.

And was stopped in his tracks.

Samuel was sitting on a chair at the kitchen table. Alarm bells started ringing. Samuel wasn't supposed to come home as soon as this. On the few occasions he had done so in the past, he'd either been ill or started drinking. But he didn't seem to be drunk. His eyes weren't red and his hair wasn't standing on end. He didn't seem to be especially ill either.

He looked up at Joel and seemed to be surprised.

'What's the matter?' Joel asked. 'Why are you at home already?'

Samuel pointed to a letter lying on the table.

'Who's it from?'

'Take your jacket off and sit down, and I'll tell you.'

Joel kicked off his wellingtons and hung his jacket over the back of his chair. Then he sat down. He was very much on edge. What could there be in a letter that was so important that it made Samuel come home earlier than usual from his work in the forest?

He noticed that Samuel was very tense. His lower lip was trembling.

'I've had a letter from Elinor,' he said. 'I haven't heard from her for ten years.'

Joel waited for what was coming next, but nothing did.

'Who's Elinor?' he asked, when the silence had been going on for long enough.

'Elinor used to run a bar in Gothenburg,' said Samuel. 'In the days when I was a sailor.'

Joel sighed silently. A few years ago Samuel had met Sara, who worked in a bar in town. Samuel had sometimes spent the night at her place. But then the relationship had come to an end. Sara had broken it off. And Samuel had started drinking. Now he had evidently received a letter from another woman who worked in a bar. Maybe Samuel had spent the night with her occasionally, as well? But why was it so important?

Samuel can be odd sometimes, Joel thought. Just as odd as all the other grown-ups. They think backwards when they ought to be thinking forwards. He gets a letter from somebody he hasn't heard from for ten years. And his lower lip starts trembling. But when I ask him how soon we can get out of this dump of a town and go to sea, I don't even get an answer.

Joel looked at Samuel, and thought that perhaps he ought to ask him something. Give the appearance of being interested.

'What does she want?' he asked.

'She's told me that she knows where Jenny lives.'

It was some time before that sunk in.

Then it seemed as if Joel had been caught up in an earthquake. He was shaking, and it seemed the house was about to collapse and fall down to the shuddering ground.

Somebody called Elinor had written a letter about Mummy Jenny. The one who had vanished ages ago and not been heard of since.

Samuel had put his glasses on.

'It says here,' he said, 'that Jenny lives in Stockholm. In a street called Östgötagatan. In a district known as Söder. And that she works as a shop assistant in a grocery store in a square called Medborgarplatsen.'

Joel stared at Samuel.

'Does it say anything else?'

Samuel took off his glasses.

'It says that she's remarried.'

'But she's married to you?'

'We never got round to getting married. So we didn't need to get divorced either.'

Joel was confused. Had Samuel and Jenny never been married?

He was interested now. He wanted to know about everything in the letter. He held out his hand. But Samuel placed his own large hand over the white paper.

'The letter's addressed to me,' he said.

'Jenny's my mum,' said Joel.

'It's written by Elinor. Elinor was a friend of Jenny's. That's why she's written to me.'

Joel tried to think straight.

'How can it say that she's remarried if she was never married to you in the first place?'

Samuel nodded slowly.

'A good question,' he said. 'But I suppose that's just what people say.'

'Does it say anything else?'

'Elinor's suffering from back pains.'

'Does it say anything more about Mum? I couldn't give a shit about Elinor.'

Joel was surprised by what he'd just said. Samuel looked at him in astonishment. Joel felt scared. Samuel could sometimes fly into a rage. Even if he used to swear himself, he didn't like it if Joel swore.

'Elinor's a nice lady,' said Samuel. 'She's worked hard all her life. It's hard going, serving in a bar. Just think about how difficult it was for Sara, the trouble she had with her legs.'

'That's not what I meant,' Joel mumbled. 'But does it say anything else about Mum?'

'No, nothing.'

'Who's she married to?'

'It doesn't say.'

The conversation petered out. Samuel put his glasses back on and read the letter one more time. Joel could see how his father's lips were forming word after word. All Joel could do was try to understand what had happened.

For the first time, somebody had been able to tell them where Mummy Jenny was living. Whenever Joel had asked about that before, Samuel had merely shaken his head and said that he didn't know.

But now, all of a sudden, everything had changed.

Mummy Jenny had an address and a job. And unfortunately, a new husband into the bargain.

Joel started to scrub the potatoes. Samuel had started reading the letter yet again.

'Can't you read it out loud?' Joel asked.

'The letter's to me,' said Samuel.

They ate their dinner in silence. Boiled potato and black pudding. They had no lingon jam left.

Joel had burnt the black pudding.

After dinner, Samuel went to his room. He switched on the radio and lay down on top of his bed. As he had closed the door of his room, Joel was forced to peep in through the keyhole. He could see that Samuel was gazing at the only photo of Jenny he still possessed.

Joel went to his room and also lay down on his bed. Grown-up people who had important things to think about often seemed to lie down on their beds to do so. As Joel was almost grown-up himself, he thought he'd better join them. But he was too restless. He got up again and went to look out of the window. It was still light out there. He tried to imagine the house where Mummy Jenny lived. Then it dawned on him that he actually possessed a map of Stockholm. He'd found it in a rubbish bin at the railway station a few years ago. The only question was: where had he put it? He started searching. And finally found it right at the back of his wardrobe. He took it to the kitchen and spread it out on the table. Samuel's door was still closed. Joel could hear music playing on the radio. He bent down and took another look through the keyhole.

Samuel was still holding the photograph of Jenny. But now he was staring up at the ceiling. Joel went back to the kitchen and pored over the map of Stockholm, trying to remember what Samuel had said. Mummy Jenny lived in a street called Östgötagatan. And worked in a grocer's shop in Medborgarplatsen.

Joel started running his finger over the map. He found Medborgarplatsen first. His heart started beating more quickly. Mummy Jenny seemed to have become more real, now that he had found the place where she worked. He kept on searching.

He had just managed to trace Östgötagatan when the door opened and Samuel came into the kitchen to join him. Joel gave a start, as if he'd been found out doing something that wasn't allowed. Maybe Samuel wouldn't want him to pin down Mummy Jenny's address? But Samuel just came to stand by his side.

'I didn't know you had a map of Stockholm,' he said in surprise.

'I found it in a rubbish bin,' Joel told him. 'I thought I'd better see if she – Elinor, that is – was telling the truth.'

'She didn't use to tell lies,' said Samuel. 'Not all that often, at least.'

Joel pointed out Medborgarplatsen. And then Östgötagatan. Samuel went back to his room to fetch his glasses. Then he pored over the map and nodded.

'She doesn't have far to go, then,' he said. 'From Östgötagatan where she lives, to Medborgarplatsen where she works.'

It suddenly occurred to Joel that there was something

he had to say. Something he couldn't overlook.

'Can't we go and visit her?' he asked. 'Now that we know where she lives.'

Samuel sat down at the table. Looked hard at Joel.

'Are you serious?'

'She might be glad to see us,' said Joel. 'After all these years. She might want to know what her son looks like. Now that he's fifteen years old and has got a good school Report. In geography, at least.'

Samuel looked doubtful.

'At least we can go there and take a look at her,' said Joel. 'Peer in through the window of the shop where she works. She probably won't be able to recognise me. And you can wear dark glasses.'

Samuel burst out laughing. That was a surprise. It was always a surprise. Samuel didn't often laugh. He often smiled. But laugh? Joel could hardly remember the last time it had happened.

'You're right, of course,' said Samuel. 'As soon as you've left school, we'll go and look for her.'

Joel wondered if he could believe his ears. Samuel realised that his son was confused.

'We'll go as soon as you finish school,' he said. 'I'll apply for a few days' holiday right away.'

'Should we write to her and tell her we're going to visit her?' Joel wondered.

Samuel thought for a moment before answering. Then he shook his head.

'She didn't tell us when she left. So why should we tell her that we're going to pay her a visit?'

Joel had another question.

'She probably won't recognise us. But the question is: will you recognise her? She might look quite different.'

'I'll recognise her all right,' said Samuel confidently. 'No matter how much she's changed.'

That evening, when Samuel had gone to bed, Joel got up again. He hadn't got undressed. He picked up his shoes and his jacket, and tiptoed out. He knew which steps to avoid, because they creaked.

It was still light when he left the house. He wheeled his bike out of the gate, then got on and started pedalling for all he was worth. He raced down to the bridge and when he eventually pulled up he was sweaty and out of breath.

He'd arrived at Gertrud's house. Gertrud didn't have a nose, and lived in a strange house in an overgrown garden on the other side of the river. Joel felt that he really had to tell her about what had happened. Gertrud was his friend. He'd already told her about Mummy Jenny who'd gone away when he was very small.

Gertrud had once undergone an operation that went wrong, and as a result she lost her nose. She didn't have many friends. Joel was one of the few.

As he leaned his bicycle against her ramshackle fence, she came out to greet him. She'd seen him coming, through the kitchen window.

'Long time no see,' she said.

'There's so much to do for school,' Joel said. 'Lots of homework.'

But that wasn't true. And they both knew it. Joel sometimes thought it was awkward, visiting somebody who didn't have a nose, and Gertrud knew that was what he was thinking.

But sometimes Joel felt he simply had to see her. Sometimes Gertrud was the only person he could talk to.

Like now, for instance. When a mum called Jenny suddenly appears out of nowhere, having been missing for so long that he can't remember what it's like to have her around.

Joel went with Gertrud into her kitchen, which was chaotic and nothing like a normal kitchen. That's the way Gertrud was. She did whatever she fancied with her furniture and fittings, made her own clothes, and paid no attention to what other people said or thought.

Joel didn't want to be seen with her in public, but it was all right to meet her here, late in the evening, in her kitchen. Besides, she gave him an opportunity to practise for the future. He'd read that when a boy became a man, the thing to do was to have secret meetings with women.

'We're going to Stockholm,' he said. 'Samuel and me. We're going to meet her. Obviously, I wonder how she's going to react.'

Gertrud thought that over, while she fitted a new handkerchief into the hole where her nose used to be.

'I'm sure she'll be pleased,' she said eventually. 'She's bound to be.'

But later, when Joel was cycling back home, it struck

him that Gertrud hadn't sounded really convincing.

Seeds of worry had been sown in his stomach.

What if Mummy Jenny didn't want to see him or Samuel? What if she was furious about Elinor having written that letter telling where she lived and worked?

It was dark in the kitchen when Joel got home. The door to Samuel's room was closed. But he wasn't snoring. He was probably still awake, thinking about the letter.

Joel went to bed. But he found it hard to go to sleep. He could picture himself and Samuel walking down a street in Stockholm.

Samuel still hadn't started snoring.

We're both lying awake, Joel thought. In our respective beds.

But we're thinking about the same thing.

A mum who's suddenly come back.

2

When Joel raised the roller blind he found that it had been snowing during the night.

The ground was totally white.

He stared out of the window, scarcely able to believe his eyes.

It was the beginning of June. Today was his last day at school. At the leaving ceremony they would sing about sunshine and joy and 'All things bright and beautiful'. And the ground was covered in snow.

A thought struck him. One he'd never had before. Perhaps it was the snow, which could sometimes fall in June, that had driven Mummy Jenny away? Perhaps she simply hadn't been able to stand it any more? All that cold and darkness and snow that wouldn't go away, despite the fact that it was summer already?

Joel shook his head in annoyance. It was a big day. His last day at school. And there was snow on the ground.

He got dressed and went to the kitchen. Samuel had already drunk his coffee. He'd also got shaved. Joel looked at him in surprise. Samuel hardly ever shaved in the middle of the week. Only if he had an appointment with the doctor, or had been summoned to the logging company's office for some reason.

Not only that, he had shaved himself thoroughly. Joel

was often irritated by the careless way his father usually shaved. There was always some stubble left under his chin.

'It snowed last night,' said Samuel with a smile. 'You never know what the weather's going to do in these parts.'

'But what you do know is that you shouldn't live here,' said Joel, making no attempt to disguise his annoyance.

'I've taken the day off,' said Samuel.

'Why?'

'So that I can go to the school-leaving ceremony.'

Joel was buttering one of the three sandwiches he ate every morning. He looked at Samuel in astonishment. Had he misheard?

'Why?' he asked.

'It's a big day,' said Samuel. 'Your last day at school. I think I ought to be there, don't you?'

Samuel had never attended an end-of-term ceremony before. In the early years Joel had found it a problem. Being the only one in the class who didn't have at least one parent present for the occasion. Then he'd got used to it, and didn't bother any more.

Joel tried to assess quickly what the implications were. Was it a good or a bad thing? He decided it was good, because Samuel had shaved properly for once. He actually felt pleased. Ever since that letter had come from Elinor, something had changed. It wasn't just that they would sit in the evening and talk about Mummy Jenny and the trip they were going to make in only a few more days' time. But Samuel knew that Joel wasn't thinking about anything else. And Joel knew that the same applied to Samuel.

'You shouldn't arrive before ten o'clock. We shall be rehearsing until then. And tidying up the classroom.'

He ought really to have picked some flowers the previous evening, but he hadn't got round to it. Two cars had crashed at the corner of Kyrkogatan and Snällmans väg. Joel had been close by at the time, and watched with interest how the two drivers had started arguing. Joel walked over to the window and stood on tiptoe. He could see a few yellow flowers under a tree where they'd been sheltered from the snow.

Joel ate his sandwiches and brushed his teeth. Then he remembered that he ought to have put on his best shirt and a different pair of trousers in view of the forthcoming ceremony. When he returned to the kitchen he realised that he would have to hurry if he didn't want to arrive late.

Samuel was sitting at the table, looking at him.

'Perhaps we ought to take a present,' he said.

Joel didn't understand what he meant at first. A present for whom? For the teachers?

Then he realised that his father meant a present for Jenny, of course. Joel hadn't thought about that.

'We must have something to take with us,' Samuel said. 'Get a move on or you'll be late for school.'

Joel thundered down the stairs. Sometimes Samuel could surprise him. Of course they must take a present for Mummy Jenny.

He was already in the street before he remembered the flowers. He leaned his bike against the fence and ran back into the garden. Seven drooping cowslips would have to do. He added a few straws of grass to make the bunch look a bit bigger. On the way to school he thought about what they could give Jenny. But he found it hard to concentrate. He would have to get the school-leaving ceremony out of the way first.

He entered the classroom at the very last moment. Miss Nederström looked disapprovingly at him. But she didn't say anything. It was the last day. Then they would all go their different ways. Miss Nederström could just as easily become emotional as she could get angry. Today she certainly wasn't going to quarrel with Joel nor anybody else.

By ten o'clock the classroom had been tidied up and decorated. The parents were squashed in at the back. Joel had noticed Samuel when he arrived: he was trapped in a corner now. Miss Nederström was in a good mood and only asked questions she knew her pupils could answer. Joel was asked a geography question. After the demonstration lesson they sang a hymn and then processed to the church, class by class. The snow had melted away by then. When they were all assembled in the church, the headmaster gave a speech, all the pupils were given their Reports, and then it was all over. Miss Nederström had tears in her eyes when she shook Joel's hand. He felt most embarrassed.

'You ought to have gone on to college,' she said.

'I've got other things I have to do first,' Joel replied.

He'd been thinking about that for nearly a year now. If he ought to try and get a place at college. But the thought of four more years' schooling was too much for him. He wanted to get out. Out into the world.

Samuel was waiting for him outside the church.

'I'm pleased that you could give the right answer to the question you were asked,' Samuel said.

'It's just as well she didn't ask me a question about history,' Joel said. 'I'd have been bound to get it wrong.'

Then they went home. Just for once, Joel also had a cup of coffee. He still wasn't quite sure what it felt like, having finished school. Knowing that after the holidays, when autumn came, there would no longer be a teacher checking up on whether he got to school on time.

Now life was going to begin. Real life. And it would start with the trip to Stockholm he and Samuel were going to make. He wasn't at all sure what would happen after that. He'd been given a half promise of a job as errand boy at the ironmonger's. But what then? What would he do next? It all depended on Samuel. Were they going to move house, or weren't they?

Joel had worked out a plan. There was a big harbour in Stockholm. Ships from all over the world went there. It wasn't as big a port as Gothenburg, but even so: perhaps Samuel would finally make up his mind. When he saw all those ships berthed at the various quays. Joel had made up his mind to take Samuel to see the ships as often as possible. Naturally, Samuel had forgotten what it was like to be a sailor. How could he possibly have remembered? Living for so long as a castaway in the depths of those enormous forests, where there was no sea, only gloomy little lakes.

Samuel examined Joel's Report in detail.

'You ought to have learnt how to count better,' he said. 'But apart from that, it's good.'

Joel said nothing. Samuel was right. Maths was the most boring subject Joel could think of.

Then they started to talk about the present they were going to take to Mummy Jenny. What should they give her?

'You're the one who knows her best,' said Joel.

'She used to be very keen on hats in those days,' said Samuel tentatively. 'But maybe she isn't any more. Besides, how would I be able to go into a shop selling ladies' clothes and pick out a hat for her?'

Joel knew that Samuel and Jenny had once met at a dance.

'Maybe she'd like a gramophone record,' he suggested.

'But has she got a gramophone?' Samuel wondered. 'You can never be sure.'

'Everybody has a gramophone,' said Joel. 'Apart from us, perhaps.'

He regretted saying that the moment it had crossed his lips. Samuel didn't like to be reminded of the fact that they had so little money. It could make him very morose. Joel didn't want that to happen. Not now.

'Maybe she has the record already,' he said.

'What record?'

'The one we were going to give her.'

This conversation's getting very odd, Joel thought.

'Perhaps we could give her a gift voucher,' he suggested. 'Then she could choose for herself what she wanted to buy.'

Samuel shook his head.

'No, it has to be something real. Something you can put in a parcel. If we had an elk steak we could have given her that.'

Joel looked at Samuel in astonishment.

'Are you saying we should take her an elk steak? What if blood were to start dripping out of the suitcase? The police would think we'd murdered somebody.'

'It's not the elk-hunting season now anyway. We'll have to think of something else.'

It was afternoon. The sun's rays were streaming in through the kitchen window. Moving steadily across the wall. Until they reached the showcase containing the *Celestine*.

'Maybe she'd like to have *Celestine*,' said Joel. 'That would be something that we like as well.'

Samuel spent a long time gazing at the model ship in its case before answering.

'I suppose it was on display there when she went away,' he said. 'You might be right. Perhaps we ought to give her *Celestine*.'

They didn't make a decision. But now they had an idea, at least.

One more week before they were due to set off.

They would take the night train on Saturday evening. They'd arrive in Stockholm on Sunday. Joel had asked Samuel about all the details. Not least where they were going to stay. Samuel had said that there were cheap hotels near the railway station. Joel was also worried that Samuel wouldn't take enough money with him. But that wasn't something he could very well ask about. Instead, he made a point of going through Samuel's wallet when his dad wasn't looking. Samuel had three hundred kronor. That was a lot of money as far as Joel was concerned. But would it be enough? He didn't know.

The days passed slowly. Joel tried to go back to sleep in the mornings after Samuel had left for work in the forest, but he was far too excited to stay in bed. He got up again, ate his sandwiches and went out. No more snow had fallen, and it had become warmer as well. He didn't just cycle around town, but went for quite long rides, exploring the logging tracks. Whenever he came to a clearing where the sun's rays managed to penetrate as far as the ground, he would find a biggish rock and sit down to think. Most of all about what it would be like to meet Mummy Jenny. But also about whether he would manage to persuade Samuel to make up his mind about moving at last. And what he would do if he didn't succeed. If they came back here and Samuel carried on going into the forest to cut down trees.

One day Joel had sat down at the kitchen table and made a long list of all the jobs he knew about. Then he tried to work his way through them all, and imagine what it would be like, doing each one.

Airline Pilot Captain Joel Gustafson

That sounded tempting, of course. Visualising yourself in uniform. With nerves of steel. Making a skilful emergency landing in the middle of some desert or other. But there again, he knew that a pilot had to be able to do sums. No doubt his mark for maths wouldn't be good enough.

Surveyor Joel Gustafson

What exactly did a surveyor do? Look at things? Measure distances? Wander around by the side of ditches and logging tracks? Noting down how far it was between fences? That would bore him stiff.

He worked his way through his long list as he sat in those sunny glades, wondering what life would be like as a motor mechanic or a gamekeeper, a watchmaker or an actor. He also thought about what he had dreamt of only a year ago: becoming a rock idol. But he had accepted the fact that he couldn't sing well enough, and probably wouldn't be able to learn to play the guitar as well as was necessary.

Some of the jobs on his list he could cross out straight away. What he wanted to be least of all was a lumberjack like Samuel. Anything at all but that.

In the end he concluded that there was only one thing he really wanted to do. To become a sailor. What Samuel had been when he met Mummy Jenny. He could become a deckhand or an ordinary seaman. Start at the bottom of the ladder. Sailors worked with ropes and did lookout duty. They didn't need to be good at sums. He would never wake up in the same place as he'd gone to sleep in. The ship was always on the move. He would get to see everything that lay beyond the never-ending conifer forests. He wouldn't need to stay in this little town where there was even snow on the ground when school broke up for the summer holidays. He would only sign on for ships that were heading for warmer climes. Somewhere out there was also Pitcairn Island, and the women waiting for him in transparent veils.

Almost every day he thought about what had happened the previous year. When he discovered that Ehnström's grocery store, where he always bought food for himself and Samuel, had acquired a new shop assistant. Her name was Sonja Mattsson, and she wasn't going to stay in the town for very long. She was somehow related to the Ehnströms. Joel had made a hopeless New Year's resolution, that within the coming year he would see a naked woman. And one day he had caught a glimpse of Sonja Mattsson wearing nothing but a transparent veil.

Then it dawned on Joel that Sonja Mattsson had gone back to Stockholm: maybe he would be able to meet her there? She had said she'd like him to visit her if he ever went to the capital. But he didn't have her address.

That thought struck him while he was sitting in a woodland clearing, crossing out jobs on his long list of possibilities. He immediately jumped into action.

Cycled back to town. He knew that if he went to the telegraph office he would be able to find out details of any addresses and telephone numbers he needed. He was a bit worried as he walked up the stairs to the office. A few years ago he had connected lots of lines at the switchboard one night when the operator had fallen asleep. Nobody had realised that he was the one who did it. But you never knew. There were some people who seemed to be able to see straight into his mind.

He went to the hatch and rang the bell. He saw to his relief that it wasn't the same operator as had fallen asleep that night when he had made his secret visit to the exchange.

'I'd like an address and telephone number in Stockholm, please,' he said.

'Do you want to phone them or send a telegram?' asked the woman behind the hatch. She looked stern, and Joel immediately felt nervous.

'Neither just now,' he said. 'I'm going to make a call later.'

'What's the name of the subscriber?'

'Sonja Mattsson.'

'And her address?'

'I don't know.'

'But you are sure she lives in Stockholm?'

'Yes.'

'Just a moment.'

She closed the hatch. Joel waited. He read a notice on the wall that explained how much it would cost to send a telegram.

But what would he put in it?

I'm coming on Sunday by train from Norrland. Please meet me. Joel. P.S. Samuel will be there as well. My father.

That was too many words. Twenty-three of them. He tried to cut it down.

Meet the train Sunday afternoon. Joel.

That was only six words. But then she wouldn't know which train to meet. And she probably wouldn't remember him anyway.

The hatch shot open again.

'There are seven persons called Sonja Mattsson in Stockholm.'

The woman handed him a telephone directory through the hatch.

'You'll have to work out which one it is you want to contact.'

She gave him a pencil and a sheet of paper. Joel took the directory over to a table and sat down to make a note of all the addresses and telephone numbers. Five of the seven were listed as 'Miss'. The other two didn't have a title at all.

Joel wrote them all down. Then he went back to the hatch and rang the bell. He returned the directory and the pencil.

'Do you know which one it is?'

'I think so.'

The hatch closed. Joel wondered why he hadn't told the truth. That he hadn't a clue which Sonja Mattsson was the right one.

As he left the telegraph office he also wondered why

he didn't go to Ehnströms' and ask. But he didn't want to. They'd only start asking questions.

The days were long. But time passed quickly even so. On the Thursday they decided they would in fact take the *Celestine* as a present for Mummy Jenny. Samuel and Joel helped each other to lift the ship carefully out of her case and wrap her up in newspaper. Joel found a suitable cardboard box. So that was the present sorted out. Earlier in the day Samuel had been to buy rail tickets.

'I thought we could sleep on the seats,' he said. 'It would be unnecessarily expensive to splash out on sleeping car tickets.'

Joel had no intention of sleeping at all. No way was he going to sleep throughout this journey.

Saturday finally dawned. When Joel went into the kitchen in the morning, Samuel was sitting at the kitchen table cleaning up his old suitcase with a damp cloth. It was brown, and the handle had been repaired with a piece of string.

'I never thought I'd have a use for this old suitcase again,' he said.

Joel didn't like the sound of that. Did it mean that Samuel had never seriously considered leaving the place where they lived now, and going back to sea? Joel wanted to ask. But he didn't. When they were standing at the quayside in Stockholm, looking at the vessels moored there, he would ask his dad that question.

No, he wouldn't ask. He would plead. Now that they knew where Mummy Jenny lived, wasn't it time to move away at last from all the cold and snow?

Joel didn't possess a suitcase. He would have to make do with his rucksack. He didn't like that idea. People travelling to Stockholm ought to have a proper suitcase. Even if they were only fifteen years old. Samuel would certainly have been able to afford to buy a new suitcase if he'd been working as a sailor.

They weren't going to be away for long. Four days would soon pass. Joel packed his best clothes. He placed the map of Stockholm on top of everything else. Everything was ready by nine o'clock. That left another eight hours before they needed to go to the railway station. Samuel was getting shaved. Joel made sure he did a thorough job of it.

'Your chin,' he said as Samuel started to dry his face.

'My chin?' Samuel wondered.

'You still have some stubble left under your chin.'

Samuel examined his face carefully in the little mirror, then applied the razor once more.

'Is that better?' he asked.

Joel nodded. He was satisfied.

It was a quarter past four when they went to the station. Joel felt indescribably happy deep down inside. It was as if he'd only just grasped what was about to happen.

They were going to make a journey.

And they were going to meet Mummy Jenny.

3

Joel was on tenterhooks as the engine lurched and started moving. The journey had begun.

He looked out of the window and saw Stationmaster Knif waving his flag. The train gradually gathered speed. Samuel was holding on to his suitcase. They were approaching the railway bridge. There was their house. The engine thundered onto the bridge. The railings hurtled past. Joel could see the water down below, and the logs floating down to the sawmills at the mouth of the river. Samuel had stood up now and joined Joel at the window. They were over the bridge already. Now came the long curve through the part of the town on the other side of the river. And then they would be swallowed up by the vast forests. Joel had never been as far away from his home as this before, and it was still only the beginning of the journey.

Samuel sat down again. They had found a compartment to themselves.

'There's hardly likely to be anybody getting on until we get to Orsa,' said Samuel. 'That means we can stretch out and sleep here. Just as good as in a sleeping car.'

Joel sat down in a window seat. It was light and summery outside. They were already in the forest. They were travelling fast now. Tree trunks flashed past the window. There's no end to the trees, Joel thought. Samuel would never be able to cut them all down. Not even if he kept going for a thousand years.

The door opened and the conductor came in. Samuel handed him the tickets.

'Change at Krylbo,' said the conductor.

Samuel put the tickets back in his inside pocket.

'So, we'll change at Krylbo,' he said. 'But there's a long time to go before that. A whole night. And the next morning.'

When Joel grew tired of watching all the trees, he decided to explore the train. Samuel had already stretched himself out on the seat, using his suitcase as a pillow.

Joel went out into the corridor. He saw a carafe on a special shelf, and took a drink of water. Then he looked closely at a map attached to the wall. He traced the journey to Stockholm with his finger. First they would come to Orsa: by then the forests would have finished. Next would come Mora, Borlänge, and then a bit further south was Krylbo. They would change trains there. That would mean they had completed over half the trip. But there was still a long way to go to Stockholm. Joel wandered along the train. It was rather full. Quite a few people were standing in the corridor, smoking. He could hear somebody singing in one of the compartments. But his walk came to an end when he reached the first class carriages. The door was locked. He retraced his steps. The passengers who could afford to travel first class didn't want to be disturbed. Joel almost bumped into a girl as she came out of a compartment. She was about his own age. Joel could feel to his annoyance that he was blushing. He didn't want to do that. He soon returned to his compartment and found Samuel sitting up and waiting for him. They had packed enough food to last them all the way to Stockholm. Joel felt hungry. He hadn't been able to eat much earlier in the day as he'd been so nervous. He'd imagined all kinds of things happening that would cause the journey to be cancelled. Samuel changing his mind, for instance. The train failing to appear. Him falling ill. He knew that was childish. Not something a fifteen-year-old ought to be imagining. But he couldn't help being childish.

That's the way he was.

'Shouldn't we have something to eat?' he asked.

'Already?'

'I'm hungry.'

Samuel opened the bag of food. It contained sandwiches, hard boiled eggs and boiled potatoes. He also had the thermos flask with coffee and a bottle of milk. Joel ate. But Samuel wasn't hungry. The tree trunks hurtled past outside. The wheels sang over the little gaps in the rails.

Later on, when Samuel had fallen asleep with his head pillowed on his suitcase, it occurred to Joel that a journey can be boring and exciting at the same time. There seemed to be no end to the trees flashing past the window. That was boring. Like a film in which nothing happens. Nevertheless, Joel couldn't tear himself away from the window. Sometimes there was a glittering reflection from a lake. An occasional house. What was really exciting was that for every minute that passed, for every little gap in the rails the train sang over, he was further and further away from the town he'd grown up in. Doing this had always been his dream.

They were only going as far as Stockholm. Even so, that was a bit of the way to the end of the world.

Which existed even if it didn't exist.

The conductor passed by in the corridor. That was a job Joel had on his list, becoming a train conductor. But he'd crossed it out. It could never match up to being a sailor. Railway lines and a sea channel marked out by flashing buoys could never be the same thing.

Joel carefully fished Samuel's watch out of his coat pocket. Midnight already. He put it back and stretched out on the seat. He had his feet towards the window so that he could still see out.

The tree trunks streaked past.

He tried to imagine what would happen when he and Samuel met Mummy Jenny. Would she shake Samuel's hand?

And what would she do to Joel? Give him a hug? Or shake him by the hand as well?

Joel sat up. It was Elinor who had written the letter to Samuel. Not Mummy Jenny herself. Why hadn't she written? Perhaps she didn't want to meet them at all? Maybe the man she was married to would be angry? Perhaps there was some law or other that said it was forbidden for him and Samuel to visit her without announcing themselves in advance? Joel was sure that Samuel didn't know much about the law. And what did he know himself? Nothing at all.

Joel looked at Samuel. Grown-ups were strange. How could Samuel sleep so peacefully? He must be just as nervous as Joel. But he was asleep. Fast asleep, with his hands clasped on his chest.

Or was he lying there and saying a prayer?

Dear God, please make Jenny glad to see me again. And Joel. Amen.

Joel sat down by the window once more. The train was shuddering its way round a long bend. He could just make out a lake behind the trees. His face was reflected in the window. His hair was short. Almost a crew cut. But the quiff immediately above his forehead made that part of his hair stand on end. It always did that. No matter how much water he used in an attempt to make it lie down.

Maybe Mummy Jenny would think he was ugly?

I know nothing, Joel thought. That's the worst thing of all. Not knowing anything.

He lay down on the seat again. The train was shaking and lurching. He tried to count the gaps between the joinings of the rails.

Then he fell asleep.

Joel woke up when the train came to a halt. When he opened his eyes he knew immediately where he was. But when he looked at the seat opposite, he saw that Samuel was no longer there. He sat up. There wasn't a sound. He opened the door and looked out into the corridor. And saw Samuel, who had opened a window. He smiled when he saw Joel.

'Did I wake you up?'

'Why has the train stopped?'

Joel was so sleepy that he could hardly keep his eyes open.

'Maybe we have to wait for an oncoming train to pass. Or there might be a signal at red.'

'Where are we? What's the time?'

'We'll be in Orsa an hour or so from now.'

'Hasn't the forest finished yet?'

Samuel laughed.

'Nearly,' he said. 'The forest's about to come to an end. For now.'

'Is that why you're standing here? To take a last look at the trees?'

'Could be.'

Joel had the impression that Samuel wanted to be left alone. Perhaps he was thinking about Jenny?

'I'm off to lie down again,' he said.

Joel fell asleep the moment he lay down.

When he woke up it was broad daylight. The sun was shining. Samuel was sitting by the window, drinking coffee. Joel sat up like a shot, as if he had to go to school but had overslept.

'Have we come to Orsa yet?' he asked.

'We've passed there. And Mora as well.'

Joel looked out of the window. The countryside was completely different. He could hardly believe his eyes.

An enormous lake stretched out in front of him, whichever way he looked.

'Lake Siljan is beautiful,' said Samuel. 'It almost makes you think you're at sea.'

'That's what I keep saying,' said Joel. 'Why do you hang about in the forest when you really want to be at sea?'

Samuel shook his head slowly, but he didn't say anything. Joel went out into the corridor to pour himself a beaker of water.

Then they had breakfast. The train stopped at Rättvik, and an elderly couple came to sit in their compartment. Samuel moved his suitcase. The man and woman chatted away. They sounded quite different from the people back home in the little town. Joel very nearly burst out laughing. Samuel noticed, and gave him a stern look.

They got off in Krylbo and changed trains. It was a very large station. Samuel was worried about boarding the wrong train. He asked three different porters if they were on the right platform. When the train arrived, it was difficult to find any empty seats. They eventually found two, and Joel sat next to the door. He was annoyed when Samuel tried to talk to him. He didn't like Samuel talking to him when others could hear. He pretended to be asleep, and quickly fell asleep in fact.

Some of the others in the compartment got off in Sala. Samuel and Joel ate the rest of their food.

'Only four more hours to go now,' said Samuel. 'Then we'll be there.'

They were the longest four hours of Joel's life. He tried to will the train to go faster. But at the same time, he tried to make it go slower. He both wanted to get there, and not to get there.

But they eventually arrived in Stockholm. All the other passengers left the train. It was all hustle and bustle and noise on the platform. Samuel and Joel were sitting opposite each other. Each of them was clinging on to his suitcase or rucksack. The cardboard box containing the *Celestine* was on the shelf in front of the window.

Samuel suddenly looked small and unsure of himself.

He's regretting it now, Joel thought angrily. What he really wants to do is to keep sitting where he is and hope that they'll attach a new engine to the other end of the train, so that he can go back home. To his confounded trees.

'We'd better get off now,' Joel said. 'Otherwise it'll set off again, and goodness only knows where we'll end up.'

Samuel nodded.

'I suppose we should,' he said. 'We'll have to find somewhere to stay.'

Samuel had often told Joel about his visits to Stockholm, but now he was acting as if this was the first time he'd ever been there. When they came to the big station concourse, Samuel had no idea which way to go. Joel had become so hot and bothered by the masses of people that he started shouting and tugging at Samuel's overcoat. There was so much to see, so much to hear.

Samuel pointed at a bench.

'Let's sit down,' he said. 'There are so many people rushing around, you can't see where you're going.'

They sat down. Samuel was still holding tightly on to his suitcase.

Joel started to get annoyed. Or was he afraid, perhaps? Because Samuel seemed to have no control over the situation.

'Where are we going to go?' he asked.

Samuel pulled a face.

'There are some cheap hotels near the station.'

Joel felt as if he'd been punched in the stomach. It was as if he were seeing Samuel, his father, for the first time. Small and with drooping shoulders. Wearing old, worn-out clothes. Despite the fact that they were the best he had. And then that accursed suitcase. With the broken handle.

He'd never felt like this before. Not even when Samuel had been drunk and Joel had to drag him home.

But now it happened. Joel was ashamed of him.

He was ashamed of having a father like Samuel.

'Where are those bloody hotels, then?' he snarled.

Samuel looked at him in surprise.

'Yes, I swore,' said Joel. 'I'll swear as much as I like.'

Samuel seemed to notice that his son was angry. He seemed to shrink even more.

'Maybe we can help each other to find our way,' he said tentatively.

Joel was still upset.

'I've never been to Stockholm before. How should I know where the exit is?'

Samuel didn't answer. He looked round hesitantly, and then he suddenly seemed to make up his mind. Joel could see it coming. Samuel straightened his back with a little jerk, as if it was fitted with a clockwork mechanism that somebody had just wound up.

'Anyway, I need a pee,' he said, gesturing towards a notice that said 'Toilets'. 'You can keep an eye on my suitcase while I'm gone.'

Samuel stood up and walked away. Joel watched him. Noticed how he kept stopping to let people in a hurry pass by him. Joel pulled the suitcase towards him and put his hand over the broken handle. He was still ashamed. Had anybody seen him? Sitting there covering up the broken suitcase handle with his hand? Joel tried to look relaxed, but it was as if he was surrounded by a halo of light announcing that he didn't belong here.

Samuel seemed to be away for a long time. Joel became more and more irritated. He wondered if he ought to go away and leave the suitcase to look after itself. In order to punish Samuel. But what exactly was it that Joel wanted to punish him for?

Thoughts were buzzing round and round inside his head. At the same time he was trying to take in everything that was happening all around him. A voice blared out from a loudspeaker, and there was a wheezing and screeching from a locomotive somewhere.

Somebody sat down beside him on the bench. It was a boy not much older than Joel. But he was wearing a suit, and a tie, and shiny black shoes. And his hair was not cut short. His hair was combed and gelled to form stiff black waves. *The Black Wave*, Joel thought. He shuffled slightly away from the boy. I hope he doesn't say anything.

But he did, of course.

'Hi!' said The Black Wave.

'Er, hello,' said Joel.

The Black Wave eyed him curiously. Joel glanced towards the toilets. What he wanted least of all just now was for Samuel to come back.

Only a few seconds ago it would have been too late. Now, it had suddenly become too soon.

'Are you going off somewhere?' asked The Black Wave, running his hand over his hair.

'I've just arrived,' Joel mumbled.

The Black Wave didn't say anything. He just kept on eyeing Joel. Then he produced a packet of cigarettes out of his pocket.

'Do you smoke?' he asked.

'No,' said Joel.

And immediately asked himself why. It wouldn't have done any harm to accept a cigarette.

The Black Wave lit one and blew a smoke ring.

'Where have you come from?' he asked.

'From up north,' said Joel.

'I can hear that,' said The Black Wave. 'I can hear that very clearly. "From up north".' He imitated Joel's pronunciation, and burst out laughing. Not nastily. It sounded most like a smoker's cough.

'Are you waiting for somebody?' asked The Black Wave.

'I'm waiting for my dad,' said Joel.

'Where's he gone?'

'He's in the toilet.'

'So your old man's in the john, is he?' said The Black Wave. 'Maybe he's nipped in there for a crafty drop of booze.'

Joel gave a start. How could this boy know that Joel's father sometimes drank too much? And could it be true? Was Samuel in there drinking?

'I'll go and fetch him now,' said Joel. 'We're in a bit of a hurry.'

'I'll bet you are,' said The Black Wave. 'Go on then, I'll look after your things for you.'

Joel was just going to let go of the suitcase handle when he remembered that it was broken. He didn't want The Black Wave to see that.

'I expect the old man will want his suitcase,' he said. 'But you can keep an eye on my rucksack.'

The Black Wave smiled. It seemed to Joel that his luck was in – he'd met somebody who'd offered him a cigarette and was prepared to keep an eye on his rucksack for him. Now he only had two things to carry: Samuel's suitcase and the box with the *Celestine*.

'I won't be a minute,' said Joel, getting to his feet.

When Joel entered the toilets, he stopped short, looking around in confusion. There were two rows of cubicles. Most of the doors were closed. He had no idea which one Samuel was in. It seemed to him that he might just as well leave, and wait for Samuel to come when he was ready. But there again, he ought to tell Samuel that The Black Wave was sitting out there in the concourse, looking after Joel's rucksack.

Joel waited. Doors opened. He suddenly started to

wonder how much crap was flushed down all those lavatories in a single day. The thought made him want to burst out laughing.

An attendant eyed him up and down, suspiciously.

'Are you waiting for somebody?' he asked.

'Yes,' said Joel. 'My dad.'

At that very moment the door of the cubicle furthest away opened, and Samuel emerged. He didn't see Joel standing there. He went to the sink and washed his hands. He looked tired. Then he turned round and caught sight of Joel.

'Where's your rucksack?' he asked.

'Out there. Somebody's looking after it.'

Samuel frowned.

'Who?'

It occurred to Joel that he didn't know The Black Wave's name.

'You don't always have to know what people are called,' he said angrily. 'He volunteered to keep an eye on my rucksack while I went to look for you.'

'I was a bit constipated,' said Samuel. 'That happens sometimes.'

Then he looked sternly at Joel.

'Are you telling me that you've left your rucksack with somebody you don't know?'

Joel could see that Samuel's worry was genuine. That made him feel a bit worried as well.

They left the toilets.

The bench was empty. There was no sign of The Black Wave or the rucksack.

47

Samuel looked at Joel.

'Where's your rucksack, then?'

Joel could feel the tears forming in his eyes. He pointed to the bench.

'There,' he said. 'But he's disappeared. And so has my rucksack.'

'That's blown it!' said Samuel. 'You can't trust all and sundry. He's obviously nicked your rucksack.'

Joel was struggling to hold back the tears. He realised how stupid he'd been. The Black Wave had sat down on the bench next to Joel in order to try and steal the suitcase and the cardboard box and the rucksack. He'd seen immediately that Joel was in town for the first time. And what had he asked about? Are you going off somewhere? And what had Joel told him? I've just arrived. From up north.

How stupid could you get?

'We're in a bit of a mess now,' said Samuel. 'We'd better find a policeman and report this.'

'Maybe he's still around somewhere,' said Joel.

'No chance,' said Samuel. 'You can bet your life there'll be no trace of him.'

'But what use would my rucksack be to him?' Joel asked. 'There was nothing in it. Only my old clothes.'

'A good question,' said Samuel. 'But we're not going to get an answer.'

Samuel walked purposefully towards a police constable who was patrolling the concourse. He explained what had happened. Joel noticed that Samuel was different now. It was as if his back had straightened itself out. The

48

policeman escorted them to the police station. Another officer noted down everything Joel said. What the rucksack looked like. And what had been inside it.

But what the policeman wanted to know most of all was what The Black Wave had looked like.

Joel could remember him well. The shirt and the suit, the tie and the pointed shoes.

When they finished, Samuel signed a document.

'We don't have a local address,' said Samuel. 'We're only here for a visit.'

'Then you'll have to come back here to ask if we've managed to catch the thief,' said the police constable.

They went back out into the station concourse. Joel looked round.

'They'll never find him,' said Samuel. 'He's vanished.'

'My toothbrush, though,' said Joel. 'What does he want my toothbrush for?'

Samuel didn't answer.

'We'd better find ourselves a hotel now,' he said. 'And then we can try to buy you a few items of clothing.'

'I don't need anything,' said Joel.

Samuel looked him up and down, worried.

'We mustn't forget why we're here,' he said. 'And after all, we can be pleased that we still have the *Celestine*.'

They left the station and went into the street.

Joel was overwhelmed by all the traffic.

Samuel looked around to establish his bearings.

Then they started walking.

4

Samuel spotted a building displaying a hotel sign.

At that very moment it started raining.

The building was old and gloomy. It was squeezed into a block next to the railway station. Samuel stopped several times, hesitated, then started walking again with Joel a couple of paces behind him.

Joel was still fretting about being so stupid as to allow The Black Wave to make a fool of him.

All kinds of thoughts went shooting through his head.

He ought to have stayed at home.

He was too stupid to be let loose in the world.

He ought to forget all about the possibility of becoming a sailor one of these days.

He should do what Samuel had done. Become a lumberjack. Nothing else.

He ought to acquire a stoop, shave carelessly and get drunk whenever things were getting him down.

Joel was so angry and bitter that he sometimes started talking to himself aloud. Samuel turned round.

'What was that you said?' he asked.

'Nothing.'

'But I heard you say something.'

'You heard wrong.'

Samuel eyed him thoughtfully. Then they carried on walking.

They stopped outside the hotel. The building was in a bad state of repair. Patches of plaster had fallen off the façade. An upstairs window was banging in the breeze.

'This place looks good,' said Samuel, as if he were trying to cheer himself up.

'It looks awful,' muttered Joel; but he was careful not to speak loudly enough for Samuel to hear what he said.

They went into the lobby. There was a strong smell of disinfectant. A bald man with thick-lensed glasses was sitting at a desk, peering at a newspaper.

They took a double room. Samuel paid in advance for two nights.

'Will breakfast be served?' Samuel asked, as he stood with the key in his hand.

'Of course it will,' said the bald man. 'But not here.'

Joel saw that Samuel was blushing. He'd never seen that happen before.

'If I ask a sensible question I expect to get a sensible answer,' said Samuel. His voice was shaking. He was angry.

The bald man lowered his newspaper.

'If you're not satisfied you can always go and find another hotel.'

'Where can we get breakfast?' Samuel asked. 'And where can we get dinner?'

He was still angry.

'There are lots of cafés and restaurants around here.'

Joel could feel Samuel's anger brushing off onto him.

Joel took a step forward and stood shoulder to shoulder with Samuel.

'We also need to find a clothes shop,' he said. 'Somebody's stolen my rucksack.'

'First turning on the left,' said the bald man.

They went to the lift. The room they had been given was on the third floor. Samuel paused and turned round.

'One other thing,' he said. 'If we get a telephone call, we're not in.'

The bald man bowed and nodded.

They walked up the stairs.

'What was all that about?' asked Joel. 'What telephone call? Why aren't we in?'

Samuel chuckled.

'We can't have him thinking that he can treat us however he likes. If you're expecting a telephone call, people think you are on important business. People are stupid.'

'I'm stupid,' said Joel. 'I let somebody nick my rucksack.'

'You'll learn,' said Samuel. 'I've had things stolen, in the past. When I was a sailor. And had gone on shore leave in various places. You do silly things at times. And clever things at other times. That's life. You'll learn.'

It was dark in the corridor.

They eventually located room 303.

They unlocked the door and went in. Everything in the room was brown. There was a patch of damp on the wallpaper, which was also brown. Samuel looked round and went over to the window.

'At least we've got a view of the street,' he said. 'It'll do.'

Joel thought the room was fine. It was the first time he'd ever stayed in a hotel. He couldn't imagine how it could be any better. Two big beds with a table and bedside lamp between them.

'Choose which of the beds you want,' said Samuel.

Joel took the one closest to the window. From it he had a view of a rooftop.

Joel carefully unpacked the present they'd brought for Mummy Jenny. He was worried in case it had been damaged. He and Samuel examined it.

'All in one piece,' said Samuel.

Joel placed it gently on the chest of drawers.

'*Celestine* has travelled just as far as we have,' he said.

They both stretched out on their beds.

'Take your shoes off,' said Samuel. 'So that you don't dirty the cover.'

In his head Joel unpacked his invisible rucksack. No doubt The Black Wave would throw away everything he found in it. Joel's shirts, and his best trousers. Not to mention his trainers. That was the worst thing. Not having those any more.

'Don't think about the rucksack,' Samuel said out of the blue. 'That's life. It's gone.'

'I wasn't thinking about the rucksack,' said Joel. 'I was thinking about my trainers.'

They lay there in silence. It was pouring with rain now. Drops were hitting hard against the windowpane.

I'm in Stockholm, Joel thought.

I've left school. I've travelled here with Samuel. And somewhere out there in the rain is Mummy Jenny.

He turned his head to look at Samuel. His dad's eyes were closed, but he wasn't asleep.

'What shall we do now?' Joel wondered.

'Wait until it stops raining,' said Samuel, without opening his eyes.

'But it might rain for a whole week.'

Samuel didn't respond. He smiled. Joel wondered what he was thinking about. Most probably about Jenny. But were his thoughts anxious ones? Or was he angry?

Joel decided it might be easier to ask Samuel questions when they weren't at home. Perhaps it was easier to get answers to your questions when you were in a hotel room?

'What actually happened?' he asked.

Samuel turned his head and opened his eyes.

'Happened?'

'When Mummy Jenny vanished.'

'She packed a case and left.'

Joel waited for what was coming next, but nothing did.

'Is that all? Just packed a case and left?'

'Yes.'

'Surely there must be something else?'

'The suitcase was brown. She was wearing a green coat. And a red hat. I can't remember what colour her shoes were.'

'And you were in the forest?'

'I was in the forest.'

'Where was I?'

'You were downstairs in old Mrs Westman's flat. She used to take care of you when Jenny was out shopping, or taking an afternoon nap.'

'And you knew nothing about it? You hadn't seen her packing her case? Or going to the railway station to buy a ticket?'

'She took a bus.'

'Didn't she leave a letter?'

'No, nothing at all. The only thing on the table was the outside door key.'

Joel felt as if he were going round in circles. Now it was time to stop and jump into the middle. Where the important questions were.

'Had you been quarrelling?'

'No.'

One more jump now, Joel. A bit closer to the middle.

'Had you been drinking?'

There was a pause before the answer came. But come it did.

'I hadn't been drinking. I didn't drink in those days. Not when she was around. Never ever. And if she hadn't left me I'd never have started either.'

Joel was right in the middle now. He couldn't get any further in.

'Mums don't run away like that. It's dads who vanish. Not mums. Something must have happened.'

Samuel sat up on the bed. So violently that it gave Joel a start. He thought he must have said something that had made Samuel angry.

But the eyes that were looking at Joel were not angry. They were Samuel's normal eyes. Tired and perhaps a little sad.

'Do you think I haven't been wondering about that?' said Samuel. 'I've been thinking about it for thirteen years. Every single day. Why did she leave me? All I know is that she's the only person who can answer that question. And that's why we're here. I want to know. Once and for all. Why she packed her case and left us.'

'Maybe she won't want to tell us,' said Joel hesitantly.

Samuel had lain down again.

'At least she ought to explain it to you,' he said after a while. 'You're her son after all.'

The sound of a vacuum cleaner came from the corridor. Joel looked out of the window. The rain was easing off.

'What shall we do?' he asked.

'First we'll have something to eat,' said Samuel. 'Then we'll go and buy you some clothes. And then we'll go looking for Mummy Jenny.'

'I don't need any clothes,' said Joel.

'I've no intention of letting you meet your mum in scruffy old clothes,' said Samuel. 'But we don't need to buy the most expensive clobber we can find.'

The rain died away.

Soon there was just the occasional drop on the window ledge. Samuel disappeared into the corridor, looking for a bathroom where he could get shaved.

Joel was looking at a painting hanging on the wall above the chest of drawers.

It depicted a woman with large breasts sitting down under a tree, leaning against the trunk. Next to her was a man kneeling down and playing the violin.

Joel started to think about Sonja Mattsson. If only he'd known her number, he could have phoned her from reception.

But what would he say to her?

This is that idiot Joel who's come to Stockholm and had his rucksack nicked. Come and rescue me.

He banished the thought. Took another look at the picture. The woman leaning against the tree really did have very big breasts. He went to the mirror next to the door. Examined his face. From the front. Then in profile. When he turned his head he got cramp in his shoulder. He swore and shook his arm until the cramp eased off. Had another look at himself. That quiff over his forehead refused to go away. He tried to imagine himself with hair like The Black Wave. Put on a make-believe tie and black pointed shoes. Then he clenched his fist and gave The Black Wave in the mirror a punch.

Right on the nose. Broke it. Blood came pouring out.

Nobody stole Joel Gustafson's rucksack without being punished.

Joel stared at the mirror. The Black Wave disappeared. The only thing left was himself. Nobody else.

He went back to the picture hanging on the wall. Stroked the woman with his hand.

The door opened. It was Samuel coming back. Joel

gave a start and fell over backwards. Samuel gave him a funny look, but didn't say anything.

When they left the hotel it was still drizzling. Samuel looked around, doubtfully.

'It's amazing how little you remember,' he said. 'I used to visit Stockholm quite a lot. In the old days.'

'That way,' said Joel, pointing. 'That's where most people are heading.'

Joel was surprised at how big a hurry everybody seemed to be in. Where on earth were all these people going to?

When they had found a department store and Joel had seen an escalator for the first time in his life, he wondered why people were even running on that, when the stairs were moving anyway.

They eventually came to the floor with men's clothing. Both Joel and his father turned pale when they saw the price tags.

'Let's go,' said Joel. 'There must be cheaper clothes than these in other shops.'

By the time they emerged into the street it had started raining again.

Joel had started to dislike Stockholm. This wasn't how he had imagined it. Crowds of people, loud noise everywhere, high prices and rain that never seemed to stop.

And he couldn't stop thinking about his rucksack. Stockholm had sent The Black Wave to welcome him. With a sneer.

'We must have something to eat now,' said Samuel. 'I noticed a licensed café on the way here.'

They hurried through the rain and came to the café entrance. Once they were inside, Joel felt at home. The place smelled the same as the bar back home where he sometimes sold newspapers or went to fetch Samuel when he'd had too much to drink. The waitresses wore the same black and white clothes as Sara, and he recognised the stale smell of rain, wet wool and tobacco. They found an empty table and sat down. Joel was already worried that they wouldn't have enough money. A waitress brought them a menu. Joel leaned over the table to be able to read the menu. Not the choices on offer, but what they cost.

'We can afford this,' said Samuel. 'Beef stew.'

Joel didn't like beef stew. But he didn't say anything.

By the time they finished eating, it had stopped raining again. Whenever the door opened Joel could see the sun shining.

They had eaten in silence. Joel had been thinking about his rucksack. He didn't know what Samuel had been thinking about.

Samuel paid and put his wallet away in the inside pocket of his coat.

'Now we must find a decent map,' he said. 'Then we can look for the shop where she works.'

Joel was surprised.

'Shouldn't we start by looking for where she lives?'

'Lots of people go in and out of a block of flats,' said

Samuel. 'But there won't be nearly as many standing behind the counter in a shop.'

Joel could see his point.

'I thought you said you would recognise her?'

'Maybe we shouldn't be over-confident about that,' said Samuel hesitantly. 'It's best to be on the safe side.'

The only way of being on the safe side would have been not to come here in the first place, Joel thought angrily.

It was the rucksack again. And The Black Wave.

They found a bookshop that sold maps. They bought the cheapest one Samuel could find. Then they sat down on a park bench that had had time to dry out, and unfolded the map.

There was Medborgarplatsen. And here was where they were now.

'There must be a tram that goes there,' said Samuel.

But Joel had noticed something else. If they walked, they would pass by the quay where boats were moored.

'Let's walk,' he said. 'It can't be all that far. And it's not very late.'

He pointed at a clock outside a watchmaker's shop. It said seven minutes past twelve.

Samuel stood up.

'You'd better take the map,' he said. 'I don't think I'm as good at finding the way as I thought I'd be.'

Now it was Joel taking the lead. He kept checking the map to make sure they were going the right way. They soon came to the water. There was the Royal Palace, and there were bridges, hotels, museums, and most important of all, boats. But Joel was disappointed to find that there weren't any cargo ships. Small white passenger boats, the occasional fishing boat. But no big ships. No ships of the kind that would need a sailor like Samuel, or a young boy like Joel who would be signing on for the first time.

'Where are all the boats?' he wondered. 'Like the ones that you used to work on?'

'Oh, they'll probably be in the harbour at Värtahamnen,' said Samuel. 'Or in Frihamnen.'

Joel stopped dead, unfolded the map and looked up Värtahamnen. But that was miles away from where they were now.

It would have to wait until another day.

They continued on their way.

Samuel had started sweating. He couldn't walk as fast as Joel, and several times used his handkerchief to mop his brow.

Joel stopped at the corner of a street. A large open square was spread out in front of them. If the city had been a forest, they would have come to a large clearing.

'This is it,' said Joel, after checking the map. 'Medborgarplatsen.'

Samuel bit his lip. Joel found himself doing the same thing. He didn't like copying what Samuel did, but he couldn't help it.

There was a pavement café in the square. Samuel pointed at it and nodded.

'I must have a cup of coffee,' he said. 'And something cold. Meanwhile you can scout around and see if you can find the shop.'

'Shouldn't we do that together?'

'We have to find the place before we can do anything,' said Samuel. 'You'll be best at doing that on your own.'

Joel left Samuel at the pavement café.

It felt as if he were setting out on the most important reconnaissance expedition of his life. He knew that was a childish thought, but he couldn't help thinking the way he did. He *was* childish. And he'd decided he was going to stay that way for as long as he wanted to.

He suddenly stopped dead.

It had dawned on him where the limit was.

There was a river that childishness would never be able to swim over. And he would soon find himself on the bank of that river when he stood in front of Mummy Jenny and said:

Here I am. Joel.

He started walking round the square. Noticed how nervous he was. He could just make out Samuel somewhere in the background.

He was close to Mummy Jenny now. Assuming the letter from Elinor in Gothenburg was right. And it must surely be.

He continued walking round the square, looking for a grocer's shop.

He paused several times, when he thought he had seen The Black Wave.

He found himself back at his starting point, and frowned. There wasn't a grocer's shop here.

He walked all the way round again. Same result. No grocer's shop.

He was quite sure. He hadn't overlooked it.

Samuel was stirring his empty cup with a spoon. Joel joined him at the table.

'There is no shop,' he said.

Samuel looked at him uncomprehendingly.

'What do you mean, there isn't a shop?'

'You heard what I said. There isn't a grocer's shop in this square. What did it actually say in the letter?'

'That Jenny works in a grocer's shop in this square.'

'How could she know that?'

'Elinor would never write anything she wasn't sure about.'

'Have you got the letter with you?'

'I left it at home.'

'Why?'

'I know exactly what it says. I've read it so many times, I know it more or less off by heart.'

Joel didn't know where his anxiety came from, but it was suddenly there. It was as if a blast of cold wind had blown past.

He didn't know what was the matter.

But he hadn't made a mistake.

Something was very wrong.

5

The cold wind drifted away.

Then they started quarrelling. As far as Joel was concerned it was obvious that they should now start looking for the block of flats where Jenny lived, but Samuel thought they ought to wait.

'Wait for what?' Joel wondered. 'There is no grocer's shop. Perhaps there isn't a flat either.'

'Of course there is.'

As Samuel answered he beckoned to a waitress and ordered some more coffee.

'You've just had a cup,' said Joel.

'It was very weak coffee.'

'It will be getting dark by the time we find the place where she lives.'

'I think we can wait for a bit. Besides, we don't have *Celestine* with us.'

Joel could feel himself growing really angry. He wasn't sure what was causing it. There was the business of the rucksack and The Black Wave. The harbour with the cargo ships being miles away from where they were. The grocer's shop that didn't exist. Samuel and all his cups of coffee. And finally that cold wind. Anxiety. The feeling that something was wrong.

It was something to do with the letter from Elinor.

The letter he hadn't been allowed to see for himself.

'Hurry up and drink your coffee, and let's get away from here.'

Samuel didn't respond.

Joel stood up.

'I'll find the place where she lives myself.'

'Sit down,' said Samuel. 'I think we should wait until tomorrow.'

'Why do we always have to wait for everything?'

Samuel pointed up at the sky.

'It'll start raining again shortly.'

'There are trams. And there are buses.'

'Do you know which ones go where?'

'You can find out.'

Samuel put his cup down on its saucer. He tried to sound firm and decisive.

'We shall do as I say. We'll wait until tomorrow.'

They started walking back to the hotel, the same way as they'd come. Samuel first, Joel following a couple of paces behind. As they approached the Royal Palace it started raining again. There was nowhere to shelter. The rain was bucketing down. By the time they reached the hotel they were soaked through and through. After drying himself down Joel was forced to put on one of Samuel's shirts. He hung his trousers over the radiator.

Joel felt like a prisoner. Without any dry trousers, he was stuck in the hotel room.

He sat on the edge of his bed and carefully unfolded

the wet map. There was the street where Mummy Jenny lived – Östgötagatan. They had been quite close by. But Samuel had insisted on waiting.

Joel knew full well it had nothing to do with the rain.

Samuel was lying on his bed. He hadn't said a word since they got back to the hotel room. And now he'd fallen asleep. Joel had his back to him, but could hear the snores.

He didn't know where the determination came from, but before he knew where he was, he had made up his mind. Carefully, so as not to disturb Samuel, he got up from his creaky bed.

Samuel's suitcase was lying open on the floor. Joel searched through it, but the letter from Elinor wasn't there. Joel felt in all the pockets in Samuel's clothes, but it wasn't there either.

So it was true. The letter really was at home.

He looked out of the window. Just for a brief moment he felt ashamed. He hadn't believed that Samuel was telling the truth.

Perhaps the simple fact was that Samuel was nervous. He needed time to steel himself before meeting Jenny again.

But why couldn't he just explain things as they were? Why did he need to hide behind lots of coffee cups all the time?

Joel felt his trousers. They had started to dry. Then he looked at Samuel. He was asleep. His chest was rising and falling. Fast asleep.

Joel couldn't stand being cooped up in the hotel room

any longer. He put his trousers on. And his shoes, which were wet as well. He borrowed a dry pair of socks from Samuel's suitcase.

Samuel had a pencil in his jacket pocket. Joel tore off a piece of the margin of the map and wrote a note.

I've gone out. Just for a little walk. I'll find my way back.

He put the note on the table. Then he opened the door quietly and slipped out. When he came to the lobby he found the bald man sitting on his chair, asleep. The street door was open. On the wall next to the desk was a large-scale map of Stockholm. Joel traced the way to Värtahamnen with his finger. It would take ages to walk there. He felt in his trouser pockets. He had nineteen kronor in there. He made up his mind on the spot. While Samuel was asleep, he would make his way to the harbour where the big ships were berthed.

There was a bell on the desk.

I'm staying in this hotel, Joel thought. We're paying to live here.

He smacked the bell with the palm of his hand – far too hard. It made a very loud clanging noise. The bald man gave a start and dropped his newspaper. He gave Joel a very dirty look.

'It's not necessary to break the bell. I'm sitting here after all.'

Joel was a bit afraid and could feel himself blushing. That made him angry.

'I want to know how to get to Värtahamnen,' he said. 'I gave the bell a light tap, but you didn't wake up.'

The bald man eyed Joel up and down suspiciously.

He doesn't believe me, Joel thought. He'll throw us both out of his hotel.

But the man behind the desk seemed to have forgotten about the bell already.

'You need to take a tram to Ropsten,' he said. 'From Stureplan. Go all the way to the terminus.'

The telephone rang. The man answered. Joel went to the map and found Stureplan. It wouldn't take long to walk there.

It was drizzling when Joel left the hotel. But it had stopped by the time he came to Stureplan. He soon found the tram stop. He didn't have long to wait. He bought a ticket and found somewhere to sit. He got off when they came to the terminus. He could see that this was the right place. At the end of a long bridge to the left was a large cargo ship, its hatches open. Big mechanical scoops were digging down into the hold and coming up with something belching black dust. Coal, perhaps. Or possibly iron ore? Joel moved closer to it, so that he could read the name of the ship.

MS Karmas.

A gangway led from the ship to the quay. A man was leaning over the rail, smoking. He was wearing a chef's hat. Joel was unable to venture as far as the quayside because it was fenced off.

But the ship was berthed there even so. *MS Karmas*.

Waiting for Samuel and Joel.

He didn't know how long he stood there, but in his

mind's eye he could see first Samuel and then himself walking up the gangway.

Then he noticed with a start that somebody was standing beside him. It was an old man with long white hair, smoking a pipe. Joel noticed that the man had an anchor tattooed on his wrist.

'So we're standing here and dreaming, are we?' said the man with a smile.

He had hardly any teeth, but his smile was friendly.

'I'm just looking,' said Joel.

'I think you're picturing yourself walking up the gangway,' said the man.

Joel stared at him. How come that this man could read Joel's thoughts?

'You can always tell when somebody wants to be a sailor,' said the man. 'There's some kind of magnet that attracts people who long to go to sea. Once upon a time I stood on a quay dreaming, just like you. In my case it was in Norrköping.'

He knocked out his pipe and gave Joel a wink.

'I'm right, aren't I?'

'Yes.'

'What's your name?'

'Joel.'

'I'm known as Geegee. George Edward Edgar Gerald Everton Edwardsson. But that's a bit of a mouthful, so people call me Geegee. Sailors and horses are very similar, really. When it comes to the bottom line.'

'Are you a sailor?' asked Joel hesitantly.

'I used to be,' said Geegee. 'But I went ashore three

years ago. After forty-five years. I thought it would be great back on land, but in fact there's always something missing. So I come here to look at the ships. You stand here to dream about what's to come, and I stand here to dream about what used to be. That's life, I suppose.'

'My dad's a sailor,' said Joel. 'Although he's a lumberjack at the moment.'

'That's life,' said Geegee.

'What do you have to do to become a sailor?' Joel asked.

'Your dad ought to be able to tell you all about that,' said Geegee.

'But I don't want to ask him.'

Geegee nodded thoughtfully.

'That's life. That's the way it is with dads. You prefer to ask somebody else. But you have to get yourself a seaman's discharge book, and in order to get that you have to undergo a medical examination. Once you've got the necessary document, you have to go to the Seamen's Employment Exchange to find out what jobs are going. I take it you're dreaming about becoming a captain?'

'I don't know. I just want to become a sailor.'

A gurgling noise came from Geegee's pipe.

'Start from there, then. And see how things go. That's life. Some young lads want to be in the engine room, others want to be the first mate. And some lads want to be deck hands. And then there are those who can't wait to get ashore . . .'

Joel thought about what Geegee had told him. Now he didn't need to ask Samuel.

'There's the *MS Karmas*,' said Geegee. 'You can see from the flag that she belongs to the Grängesberg Shipping Company.'

'Where has it come from? And where's it going to?'

'Not "it". A ship's a "she".'

'Where has she come from?'

'England perhaps. Or Narvik. As for where she's going to? Maybe Liberia. Or possibly Belgium.'

Joel knew that Narvik was in Norway. And Belgium was in Europe. But Liberia? Where was that? He wanted to ask, but didn't want to seem stupid. So he didn't.

Geegee put his pipe in his pocket, and yawned.

'I'm getting old and tired,' he said. 'That's life. It's time I took an afternoon nap.'

He nodded at Joel, and left, his white hair fluttering in the breeze. There was so much more Joel would have liked to ask him about, but still: he now knew the most important thing – what he needed to do in order to become a sailor.

He stayed for a bit longer, watching the mechanical scoops emptying the holds.

Then he took the tram back to the hotel.

When he got to their room he found Samuel sitting on his bed, waiting for him.

'Where have you been?' he asked. 'I was worried.'

'I left a note,' said Joel. 'And now I'm back again.'

Joel didn't want to tell Samuel what he'd been up to. He wanted it to be a surprise when Samuel discovered that his son knew all about what to do in order to become a sailor.

'I fell asleep,' said Samuel. 'And I had a dream, but I can't remember what it was about.'

I expect you dreamt about trees, Joel thought. You dreamt about your axes and your saws and all the trees you haven't felled yet. But I bet you didn't dream about walking up the gangway of a ship that was about to sail to Liberia.

'Where's Liberia?' Joel asked.

'Why do you want to know that?'

'There was a man outside the hotel who said he came from Liberia.'

Samuel looked doubtfully at him.

'Have you been talking to a black man? Could he speak Swedish?'

As soon as his dad said that, Joel remembered. How could he have forgotten? He'd always been top of the class in geography. How could he have forgotten that Liberia was in Africa?

'Perhaps it was Lebanon,' said Joel. 'Or even Linköping. He was difficult to understand.'

'What did he want?'

'He was trying to sell a magazine. A Christmas magazine.'

'In the middle of summer?'

Joel realised that he'd stumbled into a totally unnecessary maze of lies. He would have to get out of it as quickly as possible.

'It was from last year. And it was cheap. But I didn't buy it.'

Samuel shook his head.

'Let's go and have dinner,' he said, getting to his feet. 'And then I thought we could go to the cinema.'

Joel was surprised. That was a first. Samuel had never suggested that they should go to the pictures together. Samuel never went to the pictures anyway.

'Why?' asked Joel.

'I thought it might be fun. Seeing as we're in Stockholm.'

'I thought we were here to look for Mummy Jenny. And to look at boats.'

'I thought that could wait until tomorrow,' said Samuel. 'If we happened to bump into Jenny, I don't think I could cope. Not until tomorrow.'

Joel understood. And he had a bad conscience. Samuel was afraid. He didn't want to wait because he was lazy, but because he really was scared of meeting Mummy Jenny again.

'OK, we'll wait until tomorrow,' said Joel.

They had dinner at the same place they'd been to earlier in the day. Afterwards they wandered down a wide street where there were lots of cinemas. Joel let Samuel choose.

'Kirk Douglas is somebody I've heard of,' said Samuel. 'That film's bound to be good.'

Joel thought it was bad. Nothing happened. The actors just hung around, talking. He found it hard to concentrate. He kept imagining he could see himself on the screen. Walking up and down a gangway.

'That was a good film,' said Samuel as they emerged into the street.

Joel said nothing.

On the way home they paused and bought a hot dog. Joel started to worry about how long Samuel's money was going to last.

When they got back to the hotel the bald man was no longer there. Instead, a fat woman was sitting behind the desk.

'Would you like a wake-up call?' she asked.

'That won't be necessary,' said Samuel. 'We'll wake up anyway.'

Samuel fell asleep the moment the light was switched off. But Joel lay awake. A streetlamp was shining into the room through a gap in the curtains. And it was so noisy. Very different from home, where everything was so quiet. Where the only sound was the creaking from inside the walls.

The beam of light from outside illuminated the *Celestine*.

What's Mummy Jenny doing just now? Joel asked himself. What's she thinking about? Not about Samuel, that's for sure. Nor about me.

She doesn't know that we are so close by.

Joel pulled the covers up to his chin and tried to sleep. But there was no sleep in him. He tossed and turned. In the end he sat up. There was no point. He got out of bed and looked at Samuel's watch. A quarter past eleven. As he walked to the window he cast a glance at the picture on the wall. The young man was still playing the violin. And the woman was still sitting under the tree. He opened the curtain slightly. No rain.

Then it dawned on him.

The night was waiting for him. He didn't know how many times he'd roamed around the streets at night on his bike, but there was nothing to stop him wandering around the streets of Stockholm on foot tonight, looking for Mummy Jenny.

He got dressed as quietly as he could, then wrote another note for Samuel. To make sure it wasn't overlooked he put it on Samuel's pillow.

I can't sleep. I'm going out. Back soon.

That's all. No times. Samuel wouldn't be able to work out how long he'd been away.

The corridor was deserted. He closed the door carefully behind him. He didn't dare to take the lift. There were carpets on the stairs, so his footsteps wouldn't be heard.

A radio was playing in reception. He paused on the stairs. Perhaps the woman behind the desk wouldn't allow him to go out? Perhaps the law said you had to be in the hotel after eleven o'clock?

He tried to work out what to do.

But the solution came of its own accord. He could hear somebody snoring. He approached the desk. The snores were louder now. He peeped cautiously over the desk. The woman was asleep on a chair, asleep with her mouth open. He crouched down and hurried to the door. If it squeaked she might wake up. He took hold of the handle and eased the door open. Not a sound.

Now he was outside. He had remembered to take the map with him. It had dried out now, but it was crumpled. Then it occurred to him that perhaps it wasn't a good idea to sneak around Stockholm at night with a map in your hand. He put it in his pocket and started walking. It was a warm summer's night. Even though it was late there were a lot of people out in the streets. A tram clattered past. He could hear music coming from somewhere or other. On the other side of the street, two men were approaching, swaying unsteadily and trying to support each other.

He passed by the Royal Palace and came to the square where he'd failed to find a grocer's shop. The pavement café was closed, the chairs and tables covered by a canvas sheet. There were fewer people about now. And not so much traffic. But he noticed a police car. He crouched down, as if trying to make himself invisible. The police car passed by. Joel stood in front of an illuminated shop window and took out the map. He found Östgötagatan. Left, right, then left again. He took a step forward. Then another. How many more metres would he have to go before he found himself standing outside Mummy Jenny's home?

He tried to act like a grown-up. It was childish to wander around in the night, looking for a block of flats where a missing mum lived. But there again, it could be a grown-up thing to do. He remembered how Samuel had gone out roaming the streets when he had been madly in love with Sara.

He turned left, then right. He could hear a man and a woman arguing about money through an open window. He would never be like that. An adult arguing about money. On a warm summer's night.

Then he stopped dead. What would happen if Samuel woke up? He might be so worried, he'd phone the police.

But then he calmed down. Samuel wouldn't do that. In the first place he never woke up during the night. And besides, he knew that Joel could look after himself.

Left again. He'd soon be there. If the map was right. If the letter from Elinor was right. If what Samuel said was in the letter was right. If everything was right.

If in fact he really did have a mother called Jenny.

He looked at the street sign.

Östgötagatan.

It ought to be number 32. He crossed over the street, so that he was on the side with odd numbers.

First a brown building, then a red one with a furniture shop. Then a brown one, and another, then a grey one.

Then he was there.

He held his breath.

The number '32' was on an oval plate over the front door, lit up by a lamp. He looked up at the façade. Nearly all the windows were dark. People were asleep. Mummy Jenny was asleep. Somewhere up there behind a window.

He put his hand over his mouth to stop himself shouting out her name.

But he would never do that. It happened sometimes that he did things without knowing why, but not anything like that. He would never stand in a street shouting out names.

The light went out in another window.

Joel decided to cross over the street. Perhaps the front

door wasn't locked? In that case he'd be able to read the names of everybody who lived in the flats.

And then it dawned on him.

He had no idea what Mummy Jenny's surname was. If Samuel had never married her, it couldn't be Gustafson.

But he could check even so. Maybe people's first names would be listed as well.

Jenny Andersen, he thought.

Jenny Svensson.

Jenny Jansson.

Jenny Jesus Mary.

Jenny Joelsson.

Jenny Jennyson.

Jenny the mum who just ran away, damn her.

Enough of that. A car was approaching. When it had gone past he would cross the street and try the door.

The car passed by.

He was just going to start walking when the door on the opposite side of the street opened.

Joel didn't move a muscle.

A woman came out.

She glanced at him. Then set off walking along the pavement.

He could see in the light from a streetlamp that she was wearing a green coat.

6

Something was hurting his arm.

When Joel looked to see what it was, he realised that he was pinching it himself. He watched the woman walking down the street. And told himself that her wearing a green coat meant nothing at all. It was thirteen years since Mummy Jenny left them. This couldn't be the same coat. There was nothing to say that this woman was Mummy Jenny. There were no doubt lots of women living in that building.

Joel was sure he was imagining things. It was always the same. Imagining things that led him to reach false conclusions.

Nevertheless, he crossed the street and started following the woman. Perhaps he would catch a glimpse of her face? Samuel always used to say that he looked so much like his mum.

She turned a corner. Joel increased his pace. He was missing his trainers now. He cursed The Black Wave, who couldn't keep his hands off Joel's rucksack.

He peered cautiously round the corner. She had stopped and was looking round. Then she crossed over the street. Her heels clicked on the paving stones. A nearby clock struck twelve. Midnight. Joel tried to think where she might be going. In the middle of the night. On her own. And she seemed to be in a hurry.

Who needed to hurry when it was turned midnight?

Now she turned another corner. Joel increased his pace again. Perhaps she would disappear through some door or other before he had a chance to see which? He peered round this corner: there she was. Still hurrying along. Heels clicking.

Joel kept on following her. As long as he didn't know for certain, this could be Mummy Jenny.

She suddenly stopped and turned round. Joel just managed to sidle into the shadows. Had she seen him? He held his breath and waited. If she retraced her steps to see who it was following her, he would run off as fast as he could. But perhaps she would scream for help? What would he do then?

He held his breath. Then he heard her start walking again. Her footsteps were getting softer. He counted to five then peeped out. Waited. Then continued following her.

They came to a square. Some young people were sitting on a bench. One of them looked like The Black Wave. But it wasn't him.

She stopped again. In front of a shop window this time. Then she set off once more. When Joel came to the window he saw it belonged to an ironmonger's.

Why would Mummy Jenny be interested in tools?

It didn't fit in.

But then, nothing fitted in.

'I don't know if it is her,' he said aloud to himself. 'I just want to see her face, in order to be sure. I just want to see if I recognise myself in her.'

He darted into the shadows once more. She had stopped.

This time she went in through a gate. Joel hurried over to the other side of the street. The gate led into a courtyard in front of a large house. It looked like a school. He could see that there was a sign over the imposing entrance, but it was too dark and too far away for him to read it. There were steps leading up to the door. He watched her open it and walk into a brightly lit hall. Then the door closed behind her. She had vanished.

Joel waited. Then he crossed the street and read what it said over the entrance.

The Autumn Light Foundation.

Joel had no idea what a foundation was. And why was it called *Autumn Light*?

There was a streetlamp close to the gate. He slunk into the shadows.

What on earth was he doing? Somebody comes out of the front door of the building where his mother might possibly live. So he follows her. When he ought really to be asleep in bed in his hotel room.

That almost gave him a bad conscience. Samuel didn't have much money. But he had paid for a hotel room, and Joel wasn't even using the bed. He made up his mind to spend as much time as possible in it the following day.

He also made up his mind to leave. But he stayed.

He made up his mind not to open the gate.

Then he opened it.

But I'm not going to go as far as the steps, he told himself.

Then he walked up to the steps. But he didn't dare to open the door. He tried to listen. But there wasn't a sound to be heard.

There was a wide gravel path surrounding the house.

I'm not going to walk along that, he told himself.

Then he started walking.

The building was very large, with lots of windows. Most of them were dark, but there were lights on here and there. Very bright lights.

Autumn Light, he thought. The light of Autumn. What kind of a building could this be?

There was a large garden at the back. He paused outside a shed. The doors were standing open, and inside were several old wheelchairs.

Curiouser and curiouser. No doubt he would have been scared stiff some years ago. But not now.

It was just odd.

He continued walking and came to a side door. He noticed immediately that it was ajar.

I'm not going to go in, no matter what, he told himself.

Then he found himself taking hold of the door handle. The door creaked. But only a little. It was light inside. He let go of the handle and the door closed.

Then he opened it again.

I can always say I'm lost, he thought. They'll hear that from the way I speak. Here's a young man who's very lost indeed. He's come all the way from the north of Sweden.

I can also say that I've been sleepwalking. And that I'm staying at a hotel, but can't find my way back.

He listened. There was a single ceiling light. Not a sound. He slipped in through the door and made sure it didn't close of its own accord. For safety's sake he placed a small twig between the door and the jamb.

There was a strange smell. Musty. Old. But something else as well. Then it dawned on him what it was. Hospital.

He remembered the smell from the time when he'd been almost killed by a bus and had to spend some time in hospital.

But how could a hospital be called anything but a hospital? *Autumn Light*? It seemed strange. He tiptoed along the corridor and came to a wide double door. He opened it carefully and peeped inside. There was a stretcher trolley along one of the walls, and next to it a wheelchair.

Now he knew it was a hospital. He listened. Somewhere in the distance he could hear a door being opened and then closed again. Then all was quiet once more. He stepped cautiously back into the corridor. How would he be able to find the woman in the green coat among all these doors? He crept along the corridor, expecting somebody to appear at any moment. He was rehearsing his excuses all the time. That he was lost, had come all the way from Norrland. Or that he was a sleepwalker who had gone astray while taking a nocturnal stroll.

All the doors looked the same. He decided to open one at random. He peeped in and could see that it was almost

83

completely dark. Just a faint light from a lamp in one corner. He went in. His eyes got used to the darkness, and he saw that he was in a room with a lot of beds.

The room was filled with snores. There was a squeaking and sighing and grinding and singing. He took another couple of paces forward, and saw that there were very old people in each of the beds.

A hospital, he thought. Or an old people's home. Or a mixture of the two.

There was a strong, pungent smell. In one of the beds was an old man who wasn't snoring. Joel suddenly had the feeling that the man was watching him through half-closed eyes.

And then he thought the man was dead.

The panic came from nowhere. Joel raced out of the room and paid no attention to the fact that the door creaked.

As he hurtled into the corridor he heard voices. A door opened and closed. The voices were getting louder. Joel turned round and ran back along the corridor. But he no longer knew which door he'd just come out of. There were lots of double doors. The voices were very close now. Joel ducked in through the nearest door. He heard footsteps going past in the corridor. Two women talking. And then all was quiet again.

The room was suddenly lit up. Joel whipped round, but there was nobody there. Then he realised that he must have brushed against the light switch with his shoulder. He was about to switch off again when he saw that he was in some kind of changing room. There were rows of lockers and benches. And there was a name on every locker door.

Mummy Jenny, he thought. If it really was you coming here tonight, your name will be on one of these lockers.

Doctor Jenny, or Nurse Jenny. Or Manager Jenny.

He started to work his way along the rows of lockers. Nearly all of them had women's names on the door. There was an Arne Bergström and somebody called Hagge K, but all the rest were women.

There was a Judith and a Johanna in the first row. Joel started to work his way through those opposite.

He'd come more or less to the middle of the row.

And then he saw the name.

Jenny Rydén.

He held his breath.

Was this his mum? Jenny Rydén?

He just knew it was. But there again...

The locker door wasn't locked. If he opened it and found the green coat hanging there, he would be sure.

He decided to leave the door closed.

Then he opened it.

The coat hanging inside the locker was even greener than he'd thought. It was the same colour as a lawn.

Jenny Rydén's coat. His mother's coat.

There was a handbag hanging from a hook next to the coat.

I could open it, he thought. There might be a purse inside it. With an address. Saying 'Östgötagatan'. There might even be something else. Making it clear if she's my mother or not.

Ever so carefully, he unhooked the handbag. It was fastened with a strap and a little silver stud.

He had the feeling that he was about to open a treasure chest that he'd been looking for as long as he could remember.

But maybe he should resist the temptation to open the bag. Samuel ought to have been there as well. Jenny was just as much his as Joel's.

But he couldn't resist it. He opened the handbag. It contained a pair of gloves. And a powder compact.

And a purse.

He put the handbag down on the floor and opened the purse.

As he did so the door burst open, and a man in a white coat was staring at Joel.

He had no way of knowing if it was Arne Bergström or Hagge K.

Joel tried to say something by way of explanation, and he even bowed to the man in the doorway.

But that was as far as he was allowed to go. The man strode towards him. Joel tried to duck, but two powerful hands grabbed hold of his arms.

'A thief,' he yelled. 'You're a thief. What are you doing in here? How did you get in? What have you pinched? How did you break into that locker? What's your name?'

The questions came tumbling out of the man's mouth. He was shouting, and red in the face.

He'll hit me, Joel thought. He's going to hit me.

When the man paused to breathe, Joel tried to say

something. But the man started shouting and yelling again. The door to the corridor was flung open. An old man wearing shabby pyjamas and carrying a walking stick was peering short-sightedly at them.

'What's going on?' he asked.

'Go back to bed, Erik.'

The man holding Joel still sounded angry. The old man looked scared, turned and left.

'I'm not a thief,' Joel said. 'I'm lost.'

'A thief,' said the man again. 'You're a thief.'

'I'm just looking for my mum.'

Joel heard the words coming out of his mouth, but he had no idea where they originated. Nevertheless, the man holding him seemed to hesitate.

'Your mum?'

'Yes.'

'What's her name?'

'Jenny.'

'There are two women working here called Jenny. What's your surname?'

'Gustafson.'

Joel realised that was the wrong answer. But it was too late. The man's grip on him tightened even more.

'There's nobody here called Jenny Gustafson. You're not only a thief, you're a liar as well.'

Joel thought he had nothing to lose. If there were two women called Jenny working here, only one of them could have the surname Rydén. If he was lucky, he would have guessed right. But even if he had guessed right, he could still be wrong. He didn't know if the woman he'd seen entering the building really was his mother.

'Rydén,' he said. 'My mum's called Rydén.'

The man let go, but only with one hand. He was still glaring suspiciously at Joel.

'What do you want her for in the middle of the night?'

Joel was thinking desperately how he could get out of this awkward situation. He was usually good at getting out of awkward situations. But on this occasion, his mind seemed to have come to a complete standstill.

'We'd better go and fetch her.'

The man started to drag Joel to the door.

That was the moment when his brain started functioning again.

'It would be better if I didn't actually see her.'

The man stopped and stared at Joel.

'I thought you just said that was why you'd come here?'

'I can explain.'

The man let go of him. But he stood guard in front of the door in case Joel tried to run away.

'I went out after she'd left for work,' said Joel. 'And then the door slammed shut behind me. I didn't have a key and didn't know how I was going to get back in. She gets angry if I'm out late at night. I thought I'd come and collect her key. Then go home and unlock the door. And then I thought I'd leave the key lying on the floor. That would make her think she'd dropped it.'

The words simply tumbled out. One after the other. Joel was amazed by the way in which he'd managed to patch together a story that sounded almost like the truth.

'You expect me to believe that?'

Yes, thought Joel. Or at least, I hope you will. So that I can get out of here.

The door opened again. It was the same old man as before.

'What's going on?' he asked.

'Go back to bed, Erik. You shouldn't be up and wandering around in the night. You'll only get lost and end up in the wrong bed.'

The old man went away.

Joel thought he'd better improve his story.

'My mum would be very angry,' he said.

The answer he received surprised him.

'You can bet your life she would,' said the man, shaking his head.

Then he turned serious again. His suspicions had returned.

'How come you speak with a northern accent? Your mum speaks with a Stockholm accent.'

Joel had no idea how to answer that one.

'It's a sort of illness,' he said, and recognised at the same time that he had just come out with the daftest thing imaginable.

'What kind of an illness?'

'It's the same as with eyes,' he said. 'You can inherit your grandmother's dialect. Or your grandfather's.'

'That's the first I've heard of it.'

'I didn't know either,' said Joel innocently. 'Not until a doctor explained it to us. Only a few weeks ago.'

The man shook his head.

'I think we'd better fetch your mum even so,' he said.

'This business seems so peculiar. What are you doing out on the streets at this time of night?'

'It's the summer holidays. And I've left school.'

The man seemed to be thinking. He was still on his guard. And very suspicious.

'I was under the impression that Jenny only had two daughters.'

Joel felt as if he'd been punched in the stomach. So it was wrong after all.

The wrong mother.

Then the man shook his head.

'I suppose I'd better believe you. Take the key. I won't say anything.'

Joel walked shakily back to the handbag and felt around in it. But he could find no trace of a key.

Even so he pretended to put something into his pocket. Then he put the handbag back in the locker and closed the door.

'How did you get in?'

'There was an unlocked door at the back.'

The man sighed.

'The caretakers are careless,' he said. 'It's always the same.'

'A thief could get in,' said Joel.

The man nodded.

'You can leave through the front entrance,' he said. 'Jenny's drinking coffee at the moment. Upstairs.'

The man escorted him to the door.

'I hope you're not having me on,' he said.

Joel could feel pangs of his bad conscience.

'No,' he said. 'I'm not having you on. It happened once before. I was forced to take a room at the Raven Hotel.'

Then he went out into the courtyard.

He could have bitten his tongue off. Why did he have to mention the name of the hotel where he and Samuel were staying? He felt like kicking himself.

But there was nothing he could do about it now. He stood in front of the gate with the make-believe key in his pocket. The key to the building his mother didn't live in. But where two daughters of a woman called Jenny Rydén were presumably lying asleep.

He felt relieved. But also dejected. Relieved at having got away. Dejected because things weren't as he'd thought after all.

Or as he'd hoped.

He knew the facts now. He really had hoped that the green coat would be the same one. The one Mummy Jenny had been wearing when she went away. But now when he thought he'd found her again, he'd only found somebody called Jenny Rydén.

He started walking back to the hotel. He felt really tired now. The clock on a church tower said turned one.

The streets were deserted. Hardly any traffic.

If I wait a bit longer I'll be completely alone, he thought. Just as alone as I've always been when I wandered around the streets at home during the night. On my bike. Looking for a dog that had gone off, heading for a distant star.

The last thing he felt like was somebody who was now fifteen years old.

He glanced up at the sky.

A drop of rain hit him in the face.

It's that dog, he thought. Sitting up there somewhere, spitting at me.

Before long it started raining properly. Joel speeded up. Then it started bucketing down. He couldn't run that fast. So he slowed down again. It made no difference. He'd be soaked through by the time he got to the hotel, no matter how fast he walked.

And needless to say, he took a wrong turning. He soon hadn't the slightest idea where he was. He didn't recognise any of the streets. It took him ages to find the right way again. He was so wet by then that his shoes were full of water.

And needless to say, it stopped raining the moment he reached the hotel entrance. He opened the door slowly. The woman was still asleep behind the desk. He walked up the stairs. When he reached the door of his room, he paused to listen. All quiet.

He opened the door carefully.

But things weren't as he'd expected. Samuel wasn't asleep.

He was sitting on the edge of the bed, holding his stomach.

His face was ashen.

And he didn't ask where Joel had been.

'I have a terrible stomachache,' was all he said. 'I think I'm going to die.'

Nothing else.

I have a terrible stomachache. I think I'm going to die.

7

Joel would look back on that night as the moment when he grew up once and for all. When he slowly opened the door of his hotel room, it was as if he were really opening the door to his future.

He left his childhood behind him in the corridor.

He would never forget it. Never ever.

Samuel sitting on the edge of the bed holding a hand over his stomach. His pyjama jacket unbuttoned. His face ashen.

And the words:

I have a terrible stomachache. I think I'm going to die.

It was several seconds before it sank in. Before he grasped properly that nothing was as he'd thought it would be. A dark room and Samuel snoring in his bed.

Instead he was sitting on the edge of the bed and was in pain.

He had so much pain that it hurt Joel as well.

And then he felt scared.

What he had felt when he'd been caught red-handed with Jenny Rydén's handbag was nothing compared to this. Now he was seriously scared. His heart started pounding, like a fist beating at a door.

'What's the matter?' he asked, and could hear his voice trembling.

Samuel shook his head.

He really was in agony. Joel could see the pain oozing out from his father's eyes, from his nose, from his tousled hair and his worn-out pyjamas.

'I woke up,' said Samuel. 'I'd been dreaming that I had a stomachache. But when I woke up I found it wasn't just a dream.'

Joel had sat down beside Samuel. He'd started to feel cold now. He didn't know if it was due to his wet clothes or because he was scared. But it didn't matter either way. The important thing was that Samuel was in pain.

Samuel was rocking back and forth. The pain came and went.

'Perhaps you ought to go to the lavatory?' said Joel.

Samuel shook his head again. Joel could see that he was in so much pain that he was sweating.

'It'll pass,' said Samuel. 'But it hurts something awful.'

They sat for a while in silence. The pain wandered back and forth between them. Joel tried to think. What could he do? What did Samuel generally do when Joel had a stomachache? Give him something to drink. Or say he should try to be sick.

'Perhaps you ought to be sick?' he said.

Samuel shook his head for the third time.

'It's not that. This is different.'

Then he lay down gingerly, holding on tight to the bed frame with one hand. Joel stayed sitting where he was. He was now so cold that he started shivering.

More than ten minutes passed. Joel counted the minutes by Samuel's watch, which was lying on the bedside table.

'It feels as if it's easing off a bit,' said Samuel.

Joel's pain immediately started to ease as well.

Samuel closed his eyes. Joel stood up carefully and took off his wet clothes. When he looked at Samuel again he saw that his dad had opened his eyes.

'Is it any better?'

Samuel nodded.

'Where have you been?' he asked. 'In the middle of the night?'

Joel realised that Samuel hadn't seen his note.

'I just nipped down into the street. I couldn't sleep.'

Samuel turned his head slowly and looked at his watch. It was past two.

'I've never understood why you always go wandering around at night,' he said. 'You've done it ever since you were a little lad. You go riding round on your bike. Or you lie down and go to sleep in a bed outside in the garden. In the middle of winter.'

Joel looked at him in astonishment.

So Samuel knew all about what Joel had always thought was a secret: that Joel went out on his bike at night and rode around the streets of the little town where they lived. He'd known about it, but never said anything.

It seemed that Samuel understood Joel's astonishment. He smiled.

'You didn't think I knew about it,' he said.

'No.'

'You didn't think I'd woken up when you crept out as quietly as you could?'

'No.'

'But I did. I wondered what you were up to, of course. But I thought it better not to ask.'

'Why not?'

'Because you always came back. I suppose I thought you must be going on one of your adventures.'

Joel wanted to ask more questions, but Samuel raised a hand to indicate that he shouldn't do. The pain was coming back.

It immediately came back to Joel as well.

They carried on like this until morning. But without Joel being able to remember how it happened, he had evidently gone to bed and fallen asleep.

And he had dreamt. It seemed as if he were running around inside himself. As if it were raining inside his head. Samuel had been trying to open an umbrella, but the umbrella turned into a bird that suddenly flapped away.

Joel woke up with a start. At first he didn't know where he was. Then it all came back to him. When he turned his head he saw that Samuel's bed was empty. He jumped out of bed in panic. As he did so the door opened and Samuel walked in. He had started getting dressed. But his braces were hanging down, which must mean he had been to the lavatory. Joel could see that he was still in pain.

Samuel sat down on the edge of his bed. He looked even more ashen now, as the morning light shone in through the gap in the curtains.

'It's only five o'clock,' he said, 'but I think I'd better go to the hospital.'

It was immediately clear to Joel that his dad must be in far more pain than he could comprehend. Samuel would never normally even consider the possibility of going to a doctor. Never mind a hospital.

'I'll come with you,' said Joel, starting to pick up his clothes which were still wet.

'No,' said Samuel. 'It'll be better if you stay here at the hotel. You never know how long it's going to take at a hospital. I'll give you some money for food. I've spoken to the woman down in reception.'

'But what can I do here?' Joel complained, realising that he sounded like a whining child.

'You'll manage,' said Samuel. 'I'll phone from the hospital if it's going to take a really long time.'

His tone of voice was very firm, and Joel could see there would be no point in protesting. He sat down on his bed and watched Samuel getting dressed. He was obviously in great pain. Every movement hurt.

'A taxi is coming to pick me up,' he said, taking out his wallet.

'I've got some money,' said Joel.

Samuel seemed surprised.

'You mean you've got some money of your own?'

'I've got fifteen kronor. That'll be enough.'

Samuel took out three ten-kronor notes and put them on the bed.

'It's better to have too much than too little,' he said. 'But you don't need to spend it all. Unless it's necessary.'

Joel helped Samuel on with his jacket.

'Is it serious?'

Samuel pulled a face.

'No,' he said. 'I'll be OK as long as I can get to a doctor.'

That told Joel that it really was serious.

Samuel was afraid. And he was a bad liar. Much worse than Joel.

Joel wanted to go down to the lobby with him, but Samuel pointed at the bed.

'You've got to get some sleep,' he said. 'I won't be away for long. And then we can go and look for Mummy Jenny.'

In fact, he's only too pleased to be able to put that off, Joel thought. But he didn't say anything.

Samuel nodded and patted him on the shoulder.

'Everything will be OK as soon as I see a doctor,' he said.

Samuel left. Joel looked at the picture hanging on the wall. The young man was playing the violin. The woman with the big breasts seemed to be looking straight at him. Her mouth was half open, as if she were saying something.

It won't be OK at all, said the woman in the picture.

The violin screeched away in the background.

'Oh yes it will,' said Joel.

Then he carefully took down the picture and leaned it against the wall. With its back to the room.

There was a lump of old chewing gum stuck to it.

Right in the middle of her backside, Joel thought angrily. Why does she have to say that things won't be OK?

Joel hung up his clothes to dry.

Then he snuggled down between the sheets again.

After a while he moved over to Samuel's bed. He tried to picture Samuel in his mind's eye. Getting out of the taxi and entering the hospital.

But he was far too tired. His thoughts ran away from him. He was soon fast asleep.

He was woken up by somebody tapping on his head. He tried to duck down under the covers, but the tapping continued. As he became increasingly wide awake, he realised that it was in fact somebody belting hard on the door. He wound a blanket round his naked body and went to open it. There was a chambermaid standing outside. She looked angry.

'It's nearly midday,' she said. 'If this room is going to get cleaned today, I need to do it now.'

Midday, Joel wondered, somewhat confused. Had he really slept for as long as that?

'I'll be back in ten minutes,' said the chambermaid.

Joel closed the door. Samuel had taken his watch with him. He started to get dressed as quickly as he could. His clothes were dry, so he must have been asleep for a long time.

When the chambermaid knocked on the door again, Joel was just hanging the picture back up on the wall. He wondered if the chambermaid would need paying. And where was Samuel? Why hadn't he come back?

The chambermaid came in and gave him a dirty look.

'How on earth can anybody stay in bed until twelve o'clock?' she said. 'But it's none of my business, I suppose.'

Exactly, Joel thought.

'There's a lump of chewing gum stuck on the back of the picture,' he said. 'But it wasn't me who put it there.'

Then he left. Before she had time to say anything.

On the way down to reception he tried to make up his mind what he was going to do. He was hungry. But where was Samuel? He could feel his fear beginning to return.

The bald man was back on duty. He nodded to Joel, and gave him a friendly smile.

'I'm sorry to hear that your dad has been taken ill.'

'He'll soon be OK again,' said Joel. 'Hasn't he rung?'

'Not yet. But it usually takes a long time at hospital.'

Joel looked at the wall clock. Ten minutes past twelve. He'd slept half the day away. But at least he'd made good use of the bed Samuel had paid for. That was some consolation. Not much, though.

'It's stopped raining,' said the man, pointing towards the window. 'I think it would do you good to get some fresh air.'

'But what if Samuel rings while I'm out?'

'I'll make a note of what he says for you.'

Joel nodded. He really did need to go out. Not least in order to get something to eat.

When he came out into the street he could feel the heat. People were dressed for summer. Many of them looked cheerful.

They haven't got a father who's ill, Joel thought glumly. And they don't have a mother who ran away either.

He went to the café where they'd eaten the previous day. Joel was pleased to see that one of the waitresses recognised him and gave him a smile. He sat down at the same table as last time. First in Samuel's seat. Then he moved to the other side.

'Where's your friend?' asked the waitress as she placed a menu on the table. It occurred to Joel that she looked like the woman in the picture. The one with a lump of chewing gum stuck to her bottom.

'He's my dad,' he said. 'He's eaten already.'

'Mashed turnips with pork,' said the waitress. 'Or herring.'

'Herring, please. And a glass of milk.'

The waitress wiped down the table and left. Joel watched her go, to make sure there was no chewing gum stuck to her black skirt.

Then he wondered why he could never bring himself to tell the truth. That Samuel had stomach pains and was at the hospital. Why had he claimed that his dad had already eaten?

He couldn't think of a suitable answer.

His head was completely empty.

When he'd finished eating and left the café, he didn't know what to do. He ought to go back to the hotel and ask if Samuel had phoned. But something told him it was too soon yet.

He started walking down the street. The night in the old people's home, the woman in the green coat, the man who had discovered him, it all felt as if it had never happened.

We should never have come to Stockholm, he thought. If that confounded Elinor hadn't written that letter, Jenny would still have been missing. Which would have been just as well.

We should never have come here. Samuel would never have had stomach pains if we'd stayed at home. Maybe all that shaking on the train ruined his stomach?

A shop window attracted his attention. There was a large map of the world hanging in it. He pressed his nose against the glass and tried to find Pitcairn Island. He found it eventually. A tiny little dot in the middle of the Pacific Ocean.

He stood for ages gazing at the map. Thinking about the *MS Karmas* being unloaded. Perhaps it had already left the dock and was heading out to sea again? Once again he could picture himself and Samuel walking up the gangway.

He dragged himself away from the shop window. It was half past one now. He'd go back to the hotel in an hour's time. Samuel might have returned by then? Or telephoned, at least?

He came to a square with stalls selling fruit and vegetables. He hesitated for a moment, then bought an apple. He sat down on a bench to eat it. There were people everywhere. And all of them were in a hurry. He wondered where they were going to. To help pass the time he tried to count the number of passers-by wearing sandals, but he soon got tired of that. Two girls sat down on the bench. They were about his own age. They were talking loudly about somebody called Knut who had done something silly. One of them looked at Joel, who felt embarrassed.

'Have you got a fag?' the girl asked.

Her voice was shrill and she spoke fast. As if it wasn't just people's legs that were in a hurry, but their voices as well.

'I've run out,' said Joel.

'Why don't you buy some more, then?'

'I shall,' said Joel, standing up.

'Hurry up, then,' screeched the girl. 'What's your name?'

'Rickard,' said Joel.

Then he walked away. And didn't go back.

He tried to walk as fast as everybody else was doing, and to barge his way forward.

But he didn't know how to do it. No matter what he did, somebody always got in front of him. Beat him to the next paving stone, the next street corner, the next shop window. He was always last.

I've had enough of this, he thought. When Samuel gets back from the hospital we're either going to go back home, or to the Seamen's Employment Exchange.

The hour was up at last. Joel went to the hotel reception and looked expectantly at the bald man, who shook his head ruefully. Samuel hadn't rung.

'It always takes time at hospital,' he said. 'You have to be patient.'

Joel decided to walk up the stairs, and did so slowly. It was like climbing up an incredibly high mountain.

Every step needed all his strength. When he came to the room, the door was locked. The chambermaid had obviously left the key at reception. But why hadn't the bald man said anything?

Joel hurtled down the stairs. Just as he reached the desk, the man behind it remembered.

'You forgot the key,' he said.

Who forgot it? Joel wondered. You or me?

He trudged up the stairs again. To make it easier he imagined that he was really clambering up some steep cliffs.

He unlocked the door. Remembered what had happened during the night. Pictured Samuel sitting on the bed, clutching his stomach.

He lay down on his bed and stared up at the ceiling.

Then he checked to see if the chambermaid had removed the chewing gum.

She hadn't.

Then he pulled down the blind.

Stood in front of the mirror and thought he looked like the very devil.

Back to his bed again. Now the girl with the shrill voice was sitting on the edge of the bed. Wondering if he had any fags.

He tried to imitate her voice.

Then she lay down next to him. For the first time since he'd woken up, several minutes passed without him thinking about Samuel.

There was a knock on the door.

Joel leapt out of bed.

Samuel, he thought.

But when he opened the door, it was the chamber-maid.

'You're wanted on the telephone,' she said.

Joel flew downstairs. But he had no control over the propellers or the wings, and just as he was about to land in reception he tripped over the edge of a carpet and flew headlong over the floor. He knocked over a pile of suitcases belonging to a newly arrived traveller. The bald man burst out laughing and pointed to a little booth with a telephone. Joel closed the door behind him, took a deep breath and picked up the receiver.

'Joel here,' he said. 'Where are you? How are you? When are you coming? I'm here at the hotel, waiting for you.'

There was no answer. All he heard was a little click. The line went dead. He shouted in vain at the receiver. But Samuel wasn't there. Nobody was there. He replaced the receiver and went back to the desk.

'There was nobody there,' he said.

'Really?'

'What did he say?'

'Who?'

'Samuel. My father.'

'It was a woman asking for you. Presumably a nurse.'

'But why was I cut off?'

'It happens. No doubt they'll ring again.'

Joel sat down to wait. After half an hour he gave up and went back up the stairs.

They weren't a mountain any longer.

They were an abyss.

He lay down on the bed to wait. Then he got up, took Samuel's penknife and scraped the chewing gum off the back of the picture.

'Don't say anything,' he said to the woman in the painting.

Then he hung it up again.

He went down the corridor to the toilet.

When he came back he couldn't be bothered to lie down again.

He tried to improve the repair to the broken handle on Samuel's suitcase.

In the end it came off altogether.

Just then there was another knock on the door.

Joel leapt to his feet.

Opened the door.

There was a woman standing outside. Wearing a blue jacket.

But Joel recognised her immediately.

Despite the fact that the night before, she had been wearing a green coat when she emerged from the front door of Östgötagatan 32.

8

Joel searched.

He searched frantically. He eventually thought he'd found what he was looking for. Around her eyes. They were similar to his.

But he was staring at her in horror. When he looked back later, he could distinctly remember thinking that this wasn't how he'd imagined it was going to happen. Meeting Mummy Jenny.

How many times had he experienced this meeting in his imagination? Conjured up the circumstances? He didn't know. He had pictured them meeting in a street. Or on a beach. Or in the depths of a forest.

But never like this, in a hotel called The Raven, opening a door and expecting to see Samuel standing there.

She had walked into the room and closed the door behind her. Joel was still staring at her.

'Where is he?' she asked.

Her voice was dry and tense.

That was also something Joel had wondered about many times. What was his mum's voice like?

Now he knew. Dry and tense.

'Samuel isn't here,' Joel said.

'Where is he? When will he be coming?'

Joel decided on the spur of the moment not to tell her the truth. Not to say that Samuel had stomach pains and had gone to the hospital.

'He's gone out. I don't know when he'll be back.'

Then there was a question he wanted answering right away.

'Was it you who phoned?'

'Yes. But I wanted to meet you in person rather than on the telephone.'

Well, that's one way in which we are similar, at least, Joel thought. I don't like speaking on the phone either.

She was in the middle of the room now. Joel had backed away towards the window. He was still staring at her all the time. Even so, he wasn't at all sure that he could really see her. She was a sort of mirage. Something that existed and yet didn't exist.

She sat down on the very edge of the chair. It struck Joel that she might be just as scared as he was.

'I don't know what to say,' she said, studying her hands.

Joel immediately looked at his.

Silence.

What can I say if she doesn't know what to say? Joel thought. He'd stopped staring at her now. He was embarrassed instead. He glanced surreptitiously at her as she studied her hands.

He'd always imagined that this occasion would be full of joy. When he met his mum at long last. Not a time for stares and embarrassment.

All the pictures he'd imagined had been a waste of time. Nothing had turned out as he'd expected.

He kept on looking surreptitiously at her. All the time looking for similarities. Her hair was soft and curly. Not tufty like his. Her eyes were blue, the same as his. But she was small in stature. And thin. In a way, she was like Samuel.

Then it occurred to Joel that she was also pretty. If Jenny Rydén really was his mum, he'd been lucky. He had a good-looking mother. The question now was whether she wanted a son looking like Joel.

At that moment she looked up from her hands.

'I don't know what I should say. But I suppose I ought to say I'm sorry.'

Her eyes were moist, Joel got a lump in his throat immediately.

She stood up and turned her back on him. She took a handkerchief out of her handbag. Joel recognised it from the previous night.

She turned round again. Now she was smiling. Joel could see that her teeth where white and regular. Not like his own, that seemed to point in various directions.

'I wish Samuel was here,' she said. 'But at the same time, I'm glad he's not.'

She sat down on the chair again. And looked at him. All the time she was slowly shaking her head.

Joel broke into a sweat. She doesn't like me, he thought. She'd expected something completely different.

That made him feel angry. He didn't know where the anger came from, but he had no say in the matter. He suddenly wanted to tell her about how it had been. All those years. All those thoughts, dreams, fantasies.

She interrupted his train of thought.

'You are so big,' she said. 'But you were so little then.'

'It was Elinor who sent Samuel a letter,' said Joel. 'But we couldn't find a grocer's shop.'

'I stopped working there when it closed down,' she said. 'But how did you manage to find me at Autumn Light?'

Joel shrugged. But he said nothing.

'When Arne came and told me you'd been there, I couldn't understand what he was talking about. I thought he was making it up. But when he said that you spoke with a northern accent, I realised it must be you. No matter how unlikely it seemed. And he remembered the name of the hotel. The Raven. So I rang. And now I'm here.'

'I've just left school,' said Joel. 'It was that letter from Elinor. Samuel thought we ought to come here. So that I could find out what you looked like.'

He regretted that last sentence the moment he'd said it. But she wasn't annoyed. Instead, she stood up.

'Can't we go out? It's so hot in here. And I want to talk to you on your own, before Samuel comes back. I don't even know if I want to see him.'

'Why not?'

'I don't know. So much of this is hard to cope with.'

'I think he wants to see you.'

'Really?'

'Yes.'

She shook her head again.

'Let's go out,' she said.

Joel looked at the *Celestine*.

'This is for you,' he said. 'From Samuel as well.'

He pointed.

'I remember that,' she said slowly. 'It was in the kitchen.'

'Yes,' said Joel. 'It's always been on the kitchen wall. And it's for you.'

He produced the cardboard box they'd kept it in, that had been stashed away under the bed.

'It's for you,' he said again.

'Why should it be for me?'

'We couldn't think of a better present for you,' said Joel. 'Samuel thought you should have an elk steak. But I didn't agree. And so this is what we agreed on.'

'An elk steak?'

'Yes – but to get one at this time of year Samuel would have had to go poaching.'

She burst out laughing.

'Nobody but Samuel would ever have thought of an elk steak,' she said. 'Nobody but him.'

Joel wasn't sure how he ought to interpret what she had said. Was it positive or negative? He didn't know.

She suddenly took hold of his arm. It was the first time she'd touched him. The first time he'd felt her hand. He'd been so little all that time ago that he had no memories of it at all.

It also made him feel a bit scared. Was this really his mother, standing there in front of him? This Jenny Rydén? Or could it be somebody just pretending to be his mum?

'There's such a lot I'd like to explain,' she said. 'I don't know where to start. And I don't even know if I can.'

'It doesn't matter,' said Joel. 'That's life.'

'That's what Samuel used to say: "That's life."'

Joel seemed to recall that it was really Geegee who'd said that. But perhaps it was something everybody said when they were grown up.

That's life.

She was still holding on to his arm, and more or less whisked him to the door. She was holding the cardboard box in her other hand.

'I can carry that for you,' said Joel.

She gave him the box.

Joel locked the door. Jenny Rydén pressed the button for the lift.

I'm about to travel in a lift with my mum, Joel thought. If the lift crashes and we're killed, at least I'll have met her. Assuming she really is my mum.

'Why are you called Rydén?' he asked.

The words just came tumbling out of his mouth. He ought to have bars there, just in front of his teeth, to prevent words from jumping out whenever they felt like it.

'My maiden name was Nilsson. Then I married a man whose surname was Rydén. I'm divorced now. But I've hung on to the name.'

It seemed to Joel that it was a good thing she was divorced. That meant there wasn't a man waiting for her to come home to the flat she lived in.

But it also struck him that he had just acquired two

112

sisters. Always assuming that what the agitated man in the changing room had told him was true.

'Arne said that you had two daughters.'

'Maria and Eva. Maria's ten, and Eva's nine.'

'Was Rydén their father?'

'Yes.'

They stepped into the lift. Joel could see in the mirror that his hair was all over the place.

They found themselves looking at each other in the same mirror.

The eyes, Joel thought. That's where we're similar. We have the same eyes. And we don't like talking on the phone.

He tried to work out what it meant, having just acquired two sisters. Two younger sisters. He'd suddenly become a big brother.

Everything was happening too quickly. He didn't think he could keep up.

The lift stopped.

Joel handed in his key at reception.

'We won't be away long,' said Jenny Rydén. 'In case his dad rings.'

'We still haven't heard anything from the hospital,' said the bald man.

They stepped out into the street.

Jenny Rydén was serious now.

'Is Samuel ill?'

'He had a stomachache.'

'Is that why you came to Stockholm?'

'No. But he started having stomach pains last night.'

'I hope it's nothing serious.'

So do I, Joel thought. But he didn't say anything.

They went to a park with lots of lawns, lots of gravel paths, and lots of benches. Jenny asked if he wanted anything to eat or drink. But he said no.

It was clear to Joel that he wasn't the only one having trouble in thinking of what to say. She was in the same boat.

It's not simply a case of me finding my mum. She's just found her son as well.

They eventually selected a bench to sit on. They put the box containing *Celestine* between them.

She gave the impression of bracing herself before making a big effort.

'It was so cold,' she said. 'The winters were so cold, and the nights so long, and there was so much darkness and so much forest. There was so much ice, and so many people who never said anything. And nothing to do. I thought I was going mad. In the end, I couldn't take any more. I just packed a suitcase and left.'

'You had a green coat,' said Joel.

'Yes. I had a green coat. And all the time I kept thinking that what I was doing was absolutely wrong. That I ought to have taken you with me, at least. But I couldn't. I couldn't take you away from Samuel.'

That was something that had never occurred to Joel. The possibility of her taking him with her. If she had, he'd have grown up in Stockholm. With a step-father called Rydén. And two younger sisters.

Is that what he would have wanted?

He knew the answer to that. Nothing would have been able to make him want to do without Samuel. Despite the fact that he'd always been forced to be his own mum.

'I've always been meaning to get in touch with you,' said Jenny. 'Write you a letter. Pay you a visit. But I've never managed it. Because I didn't dare.'

Joel couldn't understand why anybody wouldn't dare to send a letter. He had posted lots of letters, with stamps on the envelopes that he'd drawn himself. And he'd made up the addresses.

But he didn't say anything. Just now it seemed to make more sense for him to listen.

'But now you've come,' she said, taking hold of his arm again.

It seemed to Joel that this Jenny Rydén was extremely nervous.

He wondered if he would ever be able to bring himself to call her 'mum'.

But maybe that wasn't necessary. He could call her Jenny.

'I have to get back to Autumn Light,' she said. 'I only have a couple of hours off.'

That was a relief as far as Joel was concerned.

They went back to the hotel and said goodbye in the street outside. She held on to both his arms. Joel found that a bit embarrassing. He thought that people passing by were staring at him.

'Say hello to Samuel,' she said. 'I want to meet him

as well now. Seeing as I've discovered that you are not dangerous.'

She let go of his arms and took a step backwards.

'It's amazing, how big you are.'

'What was wrong with Samuel?'

She didn't hear his question. He'd mumbled it. And he didn't repeat it.

She took a pen and a piece of paper from her handbag. She noted down her telephone number.

'Ring me this evening. Then we can meet tomorrow. I have the whole day off.'

'I don't know how long we'll be staying here,' said Joel.

But he'd still been mumbling. Or she hadn't heard what he said again. And she didn't ask.

Then she left.

Joel watched her go.

Jenny Rydén.

When he came to reception, he was told that there was still no message from Samuel. Joel was starting to get seriously worried now. But the bald man urged him to be patient. Joel was given his key. He was hungry. But he had no desire to eat on his own yet again. When he came to his room he lay down on Samuel's bed and learned Jenny Rydén's telephone number off by heart. Then he tore the bit of paper into little pieces and threw them into the wastepaper basket.

He looked at the table. Where the *Celestine* had been standing.

Jenny Rydén, he thought. Joel Rydén. But he backed

away from that thought double quick. His name was Gustafson. Nothing else. Thoughts were racing around inside his head. What was it she'd said when they'd been sitting on the park bench? That there'd been too much forest?

He took a deep breath, and sighed. How could you abandon your son simply because there'd been too much forest?

There was so much he didn't understand, it wasn't even worth trying to do so.

He closed his eyes.

Now he could see *MS Karmas* again. Out at sea somewhere. Captain Joel Gustafson is on the bridge. They're sailing in tropical waters. Dolphins are jumping alongside the ship. Another ship is approaching. He adjusts his telescope and sees that it is a Swedish cargo boat. He zooms in on the bows and sees that the ship's name is *MS Jenny*.

He sat up. Why had there been no word from Samuel? Why was it taking so long?

He went down to reception. The bald man shook his head. Joel asked to borrow the telephone directory. There were two of them for Stockholm. After a lot of effort he succeeded in finding the Seamen's Employment Exchange, and noted down the address. He found it on the map. It was quite close by. He checked the time. If he got a move on, he might be able to get there before they closed.

When he emerged into the street, he was like everybody else.

He was in a hurry.

They were still open. He opened the door of the Seamen's Employment Exchange and went inside. The walls were covered in notices advertising various vacant jobs. A woman was sitting at a desk, filling in a football pools coupon.

'I'd like a seaman's discharge book, please.'

'Are you fifteen?' the woman asked.

'Yes.'

She passed him some papers for him to fill in.

'Two photographs,' she said.

Then she gave him yet another sheet of paper.

'The address of your doctor, please.'

'Is there no charge for this?'

'There's no such thing as a free lunch,' she said, continuing to fill in her football coupon. Joel hoped she wouldn't win anything.

Then he sat down at a table and filled in all the papers. The next day he would go to a photographer's. And to a doctor. Then he would be able to collect his seaman's discharge book.

As he made his way back to the hotel, he found himself unable to hold back his hunger any longer. He stopped at the café he'd eaten at previously. This time he didn't recognise the waitress who tossed a menu in his direction. He chose the casserole known as Sailor's Beef.

When he got back to the hotel, the bald man nodded in greeting.

'Has Samuel rung?'

'He's in your room.'

Joel raced up the stairs. He was forced to pause outside the door and get his breath back. Then he opened it.

Samuel was sitting on the chair by the window. Just like Jenny Rydén, he was studying his hands. He was still very pale.

'Where's *Celestine*?' he asked tentatively.

'I'll tell you later,' said Joel. 'What did they have to say at the hospital? Are you still in pain?'

'It's all over now. I've got medicine.'

'You must be feeling pleased, then?'

'Of course I am.'

Joel looked doubtfully at Samuel. He didn't seem the slightest bit pleased.

'What did they do?'

'What do you mean, do?'

'At the hospital. The doctors.'

'There was only one. And it took a damned long time before he turned up.'

'What did he say?'

'That I have to go back again tomorrow morning.'

'Eh? Are you supposed to report back to the hospital tomorrow morning? But you're not in pain any more.'

'They want to take some more tests.'

'Blood tests?'

'Yes.'

'Why?'

'To be on the safe side.'

'But you're not in pain any longer?'

Samuel sighed.

'They want to find out for certain what's wrong with me. So as to make sure that it doesn't come back again.'

A particular thought had gradually started belting on all the doors inside Joel's head. But he didn't want to let it out. He was resisting for as long as he could. But in the end, he couldn't keep it out any longer. The thought forced itself out of Joel's head.

Samuel is very ill. He might be going to die.

Joel took a deep breath. Samuel looked at him.

'I'm not allowed to eat anything today. They want to make their tests on an empty stomach.'

'I've already eaten.'

'What else have you been up to today?'

'Nothing.'

'The bloke downstairs in reception says that you've had a lady visitor.'

'You must have misheard him.'

'He said you went out with a female person who came to visit you.'

Joel wondered where to start.

But he didn't need to wonder for long. Samuel came to his rescue.

'The *Celestine* has vanished,' he said slowly. 'And I can't imagine you giving her to anybody but your mum.'

Joel waited anxiously for what was coming next.

'I'm right, aren't I?'

Joel nodded.

Then he started to tell Samuel what had happened.

9

Just for once, Joel told the full story, exactly as it had happened.

He left nothing out. Samuel was able to relive the whole thing, from the moment when Joel slipped out of the hotel door. He told his dad how he'd stood in the shadows outside the building where she lived, how the door had opened and a woman wearing a green coat had come out.

Samuel listened in astonishment. When Joel got to the point where he'd been standing in the changing room holding the open handbag and the door suddenly opened, Samuel seemed to give a start.

He's with me, Joel thought. He understands exactly what it felt like.

But Joel didn't say anything about his visit to the Seamen's Employment Exchange. He thought that might be too much for Samuel to take – he still looked very pale.

As Joel told his story, he kept thinking over and over again that Samuel really was very ill. But he brushed the thought aside. Stowed it away in a corner of his mind.

'This is an amazing story you're telling me,' said Samuel when Joel had run out of steam. 'But how could Jenny know that you were staying at this particular hotel?'

'I suppose I must have mentioned the name of it. The Raven. And the man who caught me in the act must have remembered it.'

'And so she phoned here?'

'Yes. I thought it must be a nurse. Because she didn't ask for you, she wanted to talk to me.'

'All these things you are recounting are making me tired. I think I'd better lie down.'

Samuel lay on his bed. Joel sat down beside him.

It used to be the other way round, he thought. Samuel used to sit on the edge of my bed: now it's me sitting on his.

'What did she think of *Celestine*?' Samuel asked after a while.

'She remembered it. From the kitchen.'

Samuel frowned.

'Could she really remember that? It's not just something you're making up?'

'No, it's really true. She remembered it.'

'And she wanted us to ring?'

'Yes.'

Samuel shook his head.

'Funny, how things turn out,' he said. 'We were going to track her down together, and knock on her door. But nothing happens the way you'd expected. Never ever.'

'I have two sisters,' said Joel. 'Maria and Eva.'

'Two half-sisters,' said Samuel.

Joel said nothing. But he didn't like the idea of having half-people as sisters.

'Their father's called Rydén. But he's not there.'

Samuel pricked his ears up.

'Where is he, then?'

'He's gone. I don't know where.'

Samuel sat up.

'Tell me what she looked like.'

Joel did his best, but he didn't think he was very successful.

'How was she?'

'What do you mean?'

'Was she cheerful? Or nervous? Or what?'

'She was nervous.'

Samuel pulled a face.

'I should think so, too.'

There was a hard edge to his voice now. Something that surprised Joel. Something hard and firm.

'The bottom line is that she abandoned you and me.'

Joel felt the need to defend her.

'She said she left because it was too cold.'

'Eh? She left because it was too cold?'

'And too much forest. And too few people.'

'That's rubbish,' said Samuel. 'Nobody abandons their child because it's cold.'

'I'm only telling you what she said. Ask her yourself.'

'I shall do, don't worry.'

Joel thought Samuel was whingeing. Why couldn't he just be pleased that Joel had found her?

'There's a lot I ought to talk to her about,' said Samuel. 'Lots and lots of things.'

'If you're going to start causing trouble, I'm not going with you.'

'I shan't cause trouble. But there are some things that need saying.'

'Such as?'

'You simply don't do what she did. And then, afterwards, not even get in touch. All those years.'

'She didn't dare.'

Samuel looked angry.

'How do you know that?'

Joel was trying to defend Jenny Rydén.

'She said so.'

'That she didn't dare to get in touch?'

'Yes.'

Samuel muttered something that Joel didn't catch.

Then there was silence.

He can't be all that ill, Joel thought. If he was, he wouldn't have the strength to get so upset.

Samuel poured out some water from a carafe and took a pill.

'How can we go and visit her tomorrow if you have to go back to the hospital?'

'That's exactly what I was thinking,' said Samuel. 'I suppose it'll be best if you phone her and have a chat.'

'You mean you want me to ring her?'

'I have no desire to talk to her on the phone.'

'Why not?'

'The way she behaved.'

'But that was over ten years ago.'

Samuel had stood up and walked over to the window. There was a pause before he answered.

'I've never liked a woman as much as I did her,' he

said, with his back turned towards Joel. 'Not Sara, not anybody. And she just ran off. When we were going to spend the rest of our lives together. One day she simply vanished. And left me to look after you on my own.'

Samuel turned round. His eyes looked moist.

'I think it's best if you phone her,' he said. 'Meanwhile, I'll think about whether I really do want to meet her again.'

Joel stood up to leave for reception.

'Didn't she ask anything about me?' Samuel asked.

'Not much.'

Samuel nodded.

'Off you go,' he said.

Joel stood in the telephone booth and dialled the number. As he listened to it ringing at the other end, he noticed that he was sweating. It was due not only to the heat inside the cramped booth, but at least as much to his nervousness.

What should he say to Jenny Rydén? And what should he call her?

But she wasn't the one who answered.

Joel had forgotten that he'd acquired two sisters.

'Maria,' he heard a girl's voice say.

Joel slammed down the receiver. It was as if he'd been bitten. If he didn't even know what to call Jenny Rydén, what on earth should he call his sisters? He'd only discovered their existence a few hours ago.

Then there was another question that had flashed in horror through his mind.

Did they know that he existed? That they had acquired a brother? Perhaps Jenny Rydén had never told them that there was a boy miles away in the far north of the country called Joel Gustafson?

What was it the man in the changing room had said? That Jenny Rydén had two daughters, but he'd never heard any mention of a son.

Joel left the telephone booth.

He suddenly felt devastated.

So she had never even mentioned that he existed.

Not only had she run away and abandoned them, and never bothered to get in touch.

She hadn't even mentioned that he existed.

Joel Gustafson was a secret. He was hidden away right at the back of a wardrobe.

His devastation turned into anger.

I've got by without Jenny Rydén for many years, he thought. I'll continue to get by in the future as well.

When I've become a sailor I shall send her a banana spider. A big, hairy spider.

With greetings. From the boy at the back of the wardrobe.

Joel sat down on a sofa in the lobby. What should he do? Perhaps it would be as well if he and Samuel forgot all about that letter from Elinor in Gothenburg?

But that wasn't a good idea either.

Joel got up wearily from the sofa and went back to the telephone booth. He counted up to ten, gave the receiver a good shaking, as if it had been an enemy of his, and dialled the number once more.

The same girl's voice answered.

'I'd like to speak to Jenny Rydén.'

'Are you Joel?'

Joel gave a start. So she did know that he existed. But how long had she known? He realised also that it was his northern accent that had given the game away.

'I'm your sister,' said Maria. 'When are we going to meet?'

'That's what I want to talk to Jenny about.'

'You do talk funny!'

You stupid little brat, Joel thought.

'Can I speak to Jenny?'

'I'll go and get her.'

Joel forced himself not to slam down the receiver again. Jenny answered. Joel explained the situation. How Samuel had to go back to the hospital the next day.

'Is it serious?'

'No. He's just going to have some blood tests. But he wonders if we can meet this evening instead.'

She thought for a moment before answering. Joel could hear Maria saying something in the background. And there was another voice as well: that must be Eva.

Good Lord, what a row they're making! Joel thought. I want peace and quiet when I'm there. I'll teach them how to behave.

'Yes,' said Jenny. 'That'll be all right. But I'd like to meet Samuel on his own first. It was such a long time ago. And I'm so nervous.'

'Where do you want to meet?' Joel asked.

'In the square,' she said. 'Where you thought the grocer's shop was. At quarter past six.'

When Joel left the telephone booth he saw that it was five o'clock already. It took at least half an hour to walk to the square. He ran up the stairs.

Samuel didn't want to go. He complained that there wasn't enough time. He needed to get ready.

'All you need to do is have a shave and change your shirt,' said Joel.

But Samuel carried on protesting. He didn't want to.

In the end he didn't have time to get shaved, only to change his shirt. Then Joel almost frogmarched him out of the room.

'I don't want to go,' said Samuel.

'Too bad. It's decided now,' said Joel.

They arrived at the square at dead on a quarter past six. There were a lot of people milling around, but Joel spotted her immediately. She was standing beside a shop window on the other side of the square. He pointed her out.

'There,' he said.

Samuel couldn't see her.

'She's wearing a blue jacket.'

Then Samuel spotted her as well.

'I'm not going over there,' he said. 'I don't know what to say.'

'She's the one who wanted to see you,' said Joel. 'You don't need to say anything at all. All you need do is listen.'

'I don't want to anyway.'

Joel thought Samuel was acting like a little kid.

'Get going,' he said. 'But don't start causing trouble. I'll wait here.'

Samuel reluctantly shuffled off. Joel ran after him.

'Put your shoulders back,' he said.

Samuel tried to straighten up.

Joel stood and watched him go. It struck him that everything had been so different once upon a time. Then Jenny and Samuel would no doubt have run towards each other.

If they hadn't done that, Joel wouldn't be standing where he was now.

Samuel was almost there. Jenny had seen him. But she didn't go to meet him, she stayed by the shop window.

Then he saw them shaking hands. He wished he'd been much closer to them. So that he could hear what they said.

He saw they were standing about a metre apart. But what were they saying? He tried to imagine, but his mind was a complete blank.

But then something happened. Samuel took a step towards her. He raised an arm. Joel's heart missed a beat. Was Samuel going to hit her?

Then he lowered his arm again. Jenny Rydén walked past him. She was walking fast. Samuel followed her. He was waving his arms about. Joel still couldn't hear what they were saying.

Then Samuel stopped. Jenny continued walking. She

was almost running. Joel was bewildered. What had happened?

That stupid idiot Samuel, he thought. He started arguing. And now she's going away again.

He didn't know who to run after. In the end, it was Samuel despite everything.

'What did you do?' Joel shouted. 'What did you say? Why did she leave? Were you going to hit her?'

'I just told her a few home truths,' said Samuel. 'I said what I've been wanting to say to her every day since she left us.'

'What?'

'It doesn't matter. Let's go back to the hotel.'

'You can go yourself.'

Samuel stopped dead.

'What did you say?'

'I said you can go back to the hotel on your own. I want to know what you said.'

'I told her I thought she was a bloody shit heap.'

Joel gaped at him.

'Why did you say that?'

'Because that's what I think. You don't abandon your son like that. You don't run away simply because you think the winters are too long. That's what I told her. But she didn't like it.'

Samuel was so upset that he was shaking.

'I said what I'd made up my mind I was going to say. Now I've finished with her. I'm not going to give her another thought. Not a single one for the rest of my life.'

'But what about me?'

130

Joel thought his voice had turned into a squeak.

'But what about me?' he said again. His voice was back to normal now.

'That's up to you,' said Samuel. 'She's your mother. If you want to meet her, do.'

Samuel set off walking. Joel ran after him and raised an arm. Just like Samuel had done to Jenny. Samuel noticed and ducked away. Then they stood facing each other in the middle of the square, staring.

'Were you going to hit me?'

'Yes,' said Joel. 'Just like you were going to hit Jenny.'

Samuel grabbed hold of Joel's arm.

'We're going back to the hotel now!' he roared. 'And when I've been to the hospital we'll take the next train home.'

Joel was completely calm.

'I'm not going with you.'

'You mean you're going to stay here in Stockholm?'

'I've been to the Seamen's Employment Exchange. I'm going to sign on with a ship. I can't wait for you any longer.'

Samuel was silent for a while.

'Hmm,' he said eventually. 'Hmm, so that's what you've done, is it?'

'It's not too late for you to do the same.'

Samuel looked thoughtfully at him.

'Maybe not. Maybe not.'

They started walking back to the hotel.

Samuel suddenly stopped dead.

'I don't regret it,' he said. 'I don't regret saying what I did to Jenny. You have to understand that. What she did to us is something I can't forgive her for. You don't necessarily have to see it the same way. Do you see what I mean?'

'No,' said Joel. 'But just now I couldn't give a toss.'

As they approached the hotel, Samuel stopped outside a bar.

'A Pilsner would be just the thing right now,' he said.

'No,' said Joel. 'It wouldn't be just the thing at all. Besides, you have to go to the hospital tomorrow without having had anything to eat or drink.'

'I don't think a Pilsner would do any harm.'

'We're going back to the hotel,' said Joel. 'No Pilsner.'

They got up early next day. Joel went to the café for breakfast and Samuel took a bus to the hospital. Joel had money from Samuel to pay the photographer, but it would be several hours before the studio opened. Meanwhile he wandered around the streets, wondering if he dared to phone Jenny. Or should he simply write her a letter?

Samuel is an idiot. Greetings, Joel.

He found it hard to make up his mind.

He suddenly noticed the girl who had asked him for a cigarette the previous day. She was sitting on a bench, by herself, reading a magazine. Joel went to a kiosk and bought four loose cigarettes. Then he approached the bench.

'It took a little while,' he said, 'so you can have four to make up for the delay.'

The girl didn't recognise him at first. Then she burst out laughing.

'You're mad!' she said.

She put the cigarettes in her pocket.

Then she stood up and walked away. Without even saying thank you.

Joel was disappointed. Despite the fact that he didn't really know what he'd expected, or hoped for.

He thought of Sonja Mattsson, who had been naked underneath a transparent net curtain.

Things will be better once I go to sea, he thought. Then there'll be no stopping me.

He went to the photography studio and had his pictures taken. Then he looked up the address of the sailors' doctor.

The waiting room was packed.

It occurred to Joel that in a way, both he and Samuel were in their respective hospitals.

And Jenny was working in a third.

He eventually got to see the doctor, who instructed Joel to take down his trousers. He then felt around Joel's groin and pronounced him fit. He was issued with a certificate, which he took to the Seamen's Employment Exchange.

They told him he should call back after a couple of days and collect his seaman's discharge book.

He was just about to leave when he heard a voice behind him say:

'*Karmas* requires a steward and an engine room assistant.'

Two men stood up and went to a hatch in the wall.

It's my turn next, Joel thought.

The problem was what Samuel intended to do. Had he been serious? Was he really considering going to sea again? You never knew with Samuel. He could change his mind whenever it suited him.

But it was possible. Maybe he really had decided he'd had enough of wandering through the forests with an axe and a saw in his hand.

In that case, what would they do with the house by the river? And all the furniture? Joel decided he couldn't face waiting any longer. Samuel would have to follow on later.

*

Joel wandered around town for a few more hours. He paused twice to buy and eat a hot dog.

Then he went back to the hotel.

No sign of Samuel yet.

But when he collected his key, the bald man gave him an envelope.

It was a letter. From Jenny Rydén.

10

The letter was short and handwritten.

Joel sat on the steps outside the hotel and read what she had written.

My dear son,

When Samuel started shouting and yelling at me in the square, it dawned on me why I'd really left all those years ago. Without saying anything.

I couldn't say anything to you. You were too small. You wouldn't have understood.

I don't want to see Samuel ever again. But you have to understand that it wasn't easy, living with him.

I just hop you and me can continue to see each other.

I'd like that.

Jenny

Joel read the letter again.

Jenny had spelt a word wrongly. 'Hop.' She really meant 'hope'.

Then he realised that there was something in the letter he could understand fully. That it wasn't easy to live with Samuel. He'd discovered that for himself.

And how had it been for Sara? The waitress in the bar back home who hadn't been able to put up with him either?

I expect it's all to do with the fact that he shaves so carelessly, Joel thought. If you're slapdash with that, you're slapdash with other things as well.

He felt his cheeks. Only down so far. But he was quite certain that he would never shave carelessly. He'd prefer to grow a beard.

Joel wondered what to do. Should he show Samuel the letter? Or should he do what Samuel had done with the letter from Elinor? Show that it existed, but not say what was in it?

He went back into the hotel. He'd noticed that there was headed paper in one of the desk drawers. And Samuel had a pen. He'd be able to write a reply to Jenny on the spot.

'I hope it was good news,' said the bald man behind the desk. Every time he saw Joel he became more friendly.

'It couldn't have been better,' Joel said.

He sat down at the desk with the paper in front of him, pen in hand. He didn't really want to use Samuel's pen when he wrote to Jenny, but he didn't have any other.

What should he write?

He read Jenny's letter once again. He could hear her voice. What had Samuel shouted at her? That she was a shit heap.

Was that something you could really say to a woman? Samuel must be a boor. Had he really been planning that for over ten years? To tell Mummy Jenny that she was a shit heap?

Joel decided once and for all that Samuel was incomprehensible. He had an incomprehensible dad. A person nobody could understand. A boor.

He was worried that he might have inherited that boorish character. That there might be aspects of it inside himself. Only seeds so far, but seeds that might sprout and grow as he grew older. Might he one day go around calling women things he shouldn't?

He knew now what he was going to write. And he would be very careful to avoid any spelling mistakes.

When he'd finished writing, he read it through.

To Jenny Rydén,

I'd like you to know that I'm not as boorish as my father, Samuel Gustafson. I never bellow. I'd love to see you again.

Greetings from Joel Gustafson

That would have to do. He hadn't made any spelling mistakes. He folded the sheet of paper and put it in an envelope, which he sealed.

He was able to buy a stamp in reception. He'd noticed a postbox in the street not far from the hotel. He went there and posted the letter.

So that was that done.

When Samuel came back from the hospital, Joel had just been out for a meal. He'd gone to a different café, but the food tasted exactly the same. He was looking at the picture of the woman leaning against a tree, and thinking about Sonja Mattsson, when the door opened.

Samuel was wearing a hat.

A grey hat with a light blue band.

Joel stared at him. The hat was drooping down a long way below Samuel's ears.

'Wherever did you find that?' he asked.

'Find?' said Samuel. 'I bought it. And it was far too dear. But I thought I had a right to treat myself to something for once.'

'And so you bought a hat?'

Samuel examined himself in the mirror.

'Isn't it elegant?'

'It's elegant. But what are you going to do with it?'

'I'm going to wear it.'

'Out in the forest?'

'When I'm in my best clothes. On Sundays.'

Joel sighed. It was just as both Jenny Rydén and he himself had established: Samuel was a totally incomprehensible person. He never got dressed up on Sundays. He never went for walks. The hat would end up on a shelf in the wardrobe. And it would stay there.

Joel changed the subject.

'What did they have to say, at the hospital?'

'They'll be getting in touch. By letter. So we can go home now.'

Samuel walked past Joel and sat down on the chair.

Joel noticed immediately that Samuel smelled of Pilsner. That meant that he hadn't been at the hospital all day. But his eyes were not shiny. So he wasn't drunk.

'Have you eaten?' Samuel asked.

'Yes. Have you?'

'No. But I'm not hungry.'

That's not true, Joel thought. Samuel tells lies just as badly as he shaves himself. He's eaten already, and he's been drinking beer. And no doubt bought rounds for lots of old men he's never seen before. I expect he also told them he was a sailor. On shore leave.

'Have you any money left?' Joel asked.

He was starting to wonder if they'd be able to pay for the hotel room if they stayed for two more nights.

'I have enough for us to get by on,' said Samuel. 'And we'll be going home tomorrow anyway.'

Joel could see that there was no point in waiting any longer. He'd have to speak to Samuel. It was a case of now or never.

'When are we going to look at the boats?'

'We can do that tomorrow. Before we set off home.'

He doesn't want to, Joel thought. All that talk about me having to finish school first, and then we could move and Samuel could become a sailor again.

All talk. Nothing but talk.

Joel took a deep breath and braced himself.

'I'm not going with you,' he said. 'I'll be collecting my seaman's discharge book a couple of days from now. Then I'm off to sea. I can't wait for you any longer.'

Samuel stared long and hard at him. It slowly dawned on him that Joel was serious.

He said nothing. He seemed to be retreating into himself.

'That's a bit of a shock,' he said eventually.

'Why? It's what I've been dreaming about for ages. And I thought we were going to go to sea together.'

'I have to wait for the letter from the hospital.'

Lucky for him that there's something he has to wait for, Joel thought. But even if there hadn't been, he'd have thought up something. Any excuse at all to delay matters.

Then Samuel seemed to get a second wind.

'This is what we'll do,' he said. 'We'll go back home tomorrow, and then we can plan everything calmly and carefully. I'll resign from the logging company. And then we'll go to Gothenburg. There's more boats to choose from there. Stockholm's nothing. It's not a good idea to sign up for the first boat you clap eyes on. Then we'll start our travels. Best would be a boat heading for South America. They are good boats. Good boats and good ports. And you have to be careful which shipping line you choose. That's the way it is. There are good boats and there are bad boats. I think that's what we'll do.'

Joel listened. He'd sat down on his bed.

He felt sorry for Samuel. Because all he said was just words. Words that would never lead to anywhere, least of all up a gangway.

Samuel didn't want to go back to sea. Or didn't dare. Or didn't have the strength. Or perhaps it was a combination of all three.

Joel felt sorry for him.

But he couldn't change his mind now. If he did, he'd become like Samuel. He'd stay up north in that house by the river. At first he'd get a job as an errand boy for the ironmonger's shop. And then? Whatever happened next, he'd stay up there. And if he eventually had any children of his own, he wouldn't even have a sea chart on which he could show them the places he'd been to when he was a sailor.

'What do you think?' asked Samuel.

'I'm not going with you. I can't wait any longer.'

Silence again. Joel waited.

'Where will you live? While you're waiting for a ship?' The answer was obvious.

'Maybe I can stay with my mum.'

Now he's said it. For the first time. Not Jenny. Not Jenny Rydén. But my mum.

Samuel said nothing for a long time.

'That means that I'll be on my own,' he said. 'I've looked after you for all these years, and now you're leaving me. And moving in with your mum.'

'I'm going to sea. With luck I might get a job on a boat without having to wait.'

'I'll be on my own,' said Samuel.

Joel could feel that it was getting difficult now. Whenever Samuel started to feel sorry for himself he could carry on moaning and complaining for ever.

'You're the one who doesn't want to become a sailor again. That's not my fault.'

'I'll be on my own,' said Samuel again.

Joel would have liked to hit him. Shout at him. But first of all Samuel would have to stop feeling sorry for himself.

Anything was better than that.

'Let's go out,' he said. 'And you can have a beer. But only one. If you drink more than one, I'll leave you to it.'

Samuel stood up.

'That sounds like a good idea,' he said. 'When you're in Stockholm, you shouldn't just sit around in a hotel room.'

They went to the usual bar.

Samuel had a Pilsner. Joel had lemonade.

There wasn't anything much to say now. The decision had been made. Both Samuel and Joel were well aware of that.

But Joel couldn't help thinking that he might just as well go back home with Samuel. How would Samuel be able to manage on his own? How would he get enough to eat? Who would do the shopping? Who would drag him home when he'd been out drinking?

Joel tried to think of a solution. But there wasn't one.

He wasn't the only one who was beginning to grow up. Samuel would have to learn how to look after himself as well.

Joel allowed Samuel to have two beers. But no more.

Then they went back to the hotel.

They lay awake for a long time.

The light was turned off. And neither of them spoke.

Samuel's train left at 15.22.

By then Joel knew that he could stay with Jenny. He'd phoned her in the morning. It was Eva who answered

142

this time, and she fetched Jenny.

She hadn't received Joel's letter, but she said yes as soon as he asked her if he could stay there for a couple of nights while he waited for his seaman's discharge book and a position on a cargo ship.

Samuel was sitting waiting on a sofa in the lobby. He had paid for the room. He'd placed his suitcase in a storage room, having first mended the handle again.

'I tried to repair it,' said Joel. 'But I made a mess of it.'

'It doesn't matter,' said Samuel. 'It's an old case. Besides, I don't do much travelling.'

Samuel didn't have a lot to say that morning. Even less than usual. But he shook his head when Joel asked if he had stomach pains.

When they'd finished breakfast they took a tram to Värtahamnen. The *MS Karmas* had already sailed. Another ship was just berthing. It was flying a flag that Joel knew was Belgian. The *MS Gent*. Joel glanced surreptitiously at Samuel. Didn't he feel the urge now? To walk up the gangway that was slowly being lowered? But Samuel displayed no emotions. It was as if his eyes were asleep.

Afterwards, in the tram, Samuel asked Joel what kind of work he wanted to do. Did he want to be on deck, or in the engine room? Or would he become a steward?

'I'll take whatever's on offer,' Joel said. 'You've got to start somewhere.'

'I always used to work on deck,' said Samuel. 'It was too hot and noisy in the engine room. I always worked on deck.'

'I'll take whatever's on offer,' said Joel again.

They got off at Stureplan, and realised they had no idea what to do next. It was a matter of waiting for several hours until the train left.

Joel was both worried and excited. All the time he was afraid that he'd suddenly change his mind.

They strolled around along the quays where the smaller boats were moored. Joel kept thinking he ought to say something. But what? And didn't Samuel have any good advice to give him?

They wandered about, dragging behind them a heavy cargo of silence.

Eventually it was time to collect Samuel's suitcase and head for the station.

When they got there Joel went to the police office and asked about his rucksack. But it was still missing. As was The Black Wave.

Samuel took out his wallet and gave Joel ninety kronor.

'That's all I've got,' he said.

Joel didn't want to accept the money. There was nothing he needed.

'You must have a change of clothes or two,' said Samuel. 'You should really have a kitbag, but you can buy one of those after you've started to get paid.'

Then they found the right platform. The train hadn't come in yet.

'You're doing the right thing,' said Samuel. 'It's right for you to go to sea. But I don't have the strength. Not at the moment.'

'I hope you can find somebody to cook for you.'

'That will sort itself out, no doubt.'

'Don't forget to add salt to the potatoes when you boil them. And don't turn the heat too high.'

Samuel nodded.

'I'll remember that.'

'When I boil your eggs I usually count up to 200. Then they turn out exactly as you like them.'

'Do you count slowly or fast?'

Joel started counting, to demonstrate. Samuel nodded. He'd bear that in mind.

'You must remember to pour some cold water into the saucepan after you've made porridge. Otherwise it will be impossible to wash it up properly.'

Samuel promised to do as Joel said. And then the train clattered in.

They shook hands. They both had lumps in their throats.

'I'll write,' said Joel. 'As soon as I know which boat I'll be sailing on.'

'I'll remember what you said about the porridge pan,' said Samuel. 'Cold water. Otherwise it'll be difficult to wash it up.'

That was all they had time for.

Samuel boarded the train. The doors were closed. Samuel had opened a window.

'Did you say it was 200 you counted up to?'

'Yes.'

The train shuddered and started to move.

Samuel nodded and raised his hand.

'I hope you aren't seasick,' he shouted.

Joel watched the train pulling out of the station.

For a moment he felt the urge to run after it and jump aboard the last carriage.

But it was too late now.

The train had already left.

Joel arrived at Östgötagatan 32 shortly after five o'clock. He'd bought some underclothes and a shirt. But no trainers. He still had forty kronor left. In his pocket was the toothbrush he'd bought that first day.

But that was all he had.

He'd dragged it out for as long as possible before coming here. He'd even wondered if he had enough money to stay at the hotel for another night.

Everything was happening so quickly. He had difficulty in keeping up with himself. It was as if his head was in one place and his body in another.

He'd also considered phoning Sonja Mattsson. But he decided not to. He didn't dare. Everything was difficult enough without that.

All the time, he was thinking of Samuel. For each second that passed, they drifted further and further apart.

He'll forget to add salt to the potatoes, Joel thought. He'll never learn how to count so that the eggs are done as he likes them.

What I really ought to do is write it all down.

A cookery book from Joel to Samuel.

For dishes that won't be all that good, but won't get burnt and stick to the pan.

But there came a point when he couldn't delay things

any longer. Jenny Rydén and her daughters were no doubt wondering what had happened to him.

He entered through the front door. The Rydéns lived on the fourth floor. There was a lift, but Joel walked up the stairs. He wanted time to prepare himself.

Now he was going to meet his sisters.

Perhaps he ought to have brought presents for them as well.

He paused when he came to the last landing before the fourth floor. He sat down.

He wished he had a hiding place. A hide that could be folded up and stuffed into his pocket. And taken out again whenever necessary.

Just now was such a moment.

He needed a hiding place here on the staircase. Somewhere to which he could withdraw, suspend time, and think through all the things that had happened these last few days.

It still wasn't too late for him to change his mind. The last thing Samuel had given him at the railway station was the return half of his ticket. If he didn't use it, he could send it back to Samuel in an envelope. Then Samuel would be able to take it to the station and get a refund.

Joel would have preferred not to have it. But Samuel insisted. Something could happen. He might change his mind.

Joel felt in his pocket. The ticket was still there.

He could take the train leaving the next day. And when Samuel got back home from work, the potatoes would be ready for him.

It was tempting.

But he forced himself: there would be no going back. In a few days' time he would be issued with his discharge book.

Until then he'd stay with Jenny Rydén. And his sisters.

Somebody came in through the front door down below.

Joel stood up. He couldn't delay things any longer.

He walked up the last few stairs and rang the bell on the door where it said *J. Rydén*.

11

It was Jenny Rydén who opened the door.

On each side of her was a little girl, peering out at him. One of them, the elder girl called Maria, had blonde hair and a round face. But Joel gave a start when he set eyes on the other girl.

There was no doubt about it: Joel and Eva were very similar. He couldn't put his finger on exactly what it was, but looking at her was like seeing his own face in a mirror.

'We'd started to wonder,' said Jenny Rydén with a smile.

She seemed less nervous now. Her voice wasn't as tense as it had been that first time.

Joel hung up his jacket and put down the bags containing his new clothes. They went into the living room. The sun shone in through the windows.

'So, these are your sisters,' said Jenny. 'Maria and Eva.'

The girls were shy, and tried to hide behind each other. Joel felt embarrassed. Should he shake hands with them? Or what?

'They've been going on and on,' said Jenny. 'Wondering when they were going to get to see their brother.'

So I haven't been a ghost hidden away in a wardrobe, Joel thought. That was a relief, despite everything. The man who caught Joel in the changing room hadn't known anything about him, but he'd been real enough for the two girls.

'There's something I want to show you,' said Jenny.

She led Joel to where several framed photographs were hanging on a wall. A man with close-cropped hair and glasses caught Joel's attention.

'Is that Rydén?'

'It's our dad,' said Maria.

'That's not the one I wanted to show you,' said Jenny.

She pointed at a photograph of a little boy lying naked on a blanket. It was black and white, and rather dark. Joel leaned forward.

'Who is it?'

'It's you. Can you see where it was taken?'

Joel looked hard at the picture. He had some difficulty in making out the background. But there was something about it he felt he recognised.

Then the penny dropped.

The picture had been taken in the kitchen at home. He could even see the *Celestine* in its case on the wall.

So it's true, he thought. Jenny Rydén really is my mum.

Once upon a time, a long time ago, she and Samuel had lived together. And I lay on the kitchen table and had my photograph taken.

'Who took the picture?' he asked.

'Samuel.'

'But surely he can't take photos? He's never even owned a camera.'

'He borrowed one. I can't remember who from.'

Joel studied the picture of himself. He was looking straight at the camera, laughing.

Joel didn't recognise himself.

The picture was from a long time ago, when he still hadn't started to accumulate any memories.

Joel examined the other photographs. There was something missing. In one place there was a faint mark on the wall, showing that there had been a picture hanging there as well.

Samuel, Joel thought. After he'd shouted and yelled at her in the square, she went home and took down the picture. But Rydén was still there.

'Now you know,' she said. 'That it really is true.'

'Yes,' said Joel.

But he didn't like that mark on the wallpaper. Just because Samuel had boiled over and shouted at her, she didn't need to take down his picture.

She showed him where he could sleep: in a little room behind the kitchen.

Then they made a tour of the flat. Joel had never seen so many toys as there were in the girls' room. As soon as he'd entered the flat he'd started to wonder how somebody who worked in an old people's home could afford to buy such elegant furniture. Perhaps Jenny Rydén was rich? But where had she got her money from? He decided it was probably the man with the close-cropped hair who'd had the money to buy all the furniture and all the toys.

He took an immediate dislike to Rydén. He thought about Samuel, who'd never had any money all his life.

He would tell Jenny to hang up the photograph of Samuel again. Not just now. But before he left them and went to sea.

Instead of mentioning the photograph, he said something that wasn't true.

'Samuel sends his greetings. He didn't mean to hurt you. He sometimes says things he regrets afterwards.'

'Oh, I know all about that! But it suddenly became too much for me.'

Perhaps it became too much for Samuel as well, Joel thought. After all, more than ten years had passed without him even knowing where you lived.

They'd returned to the living room. The girls were with them all the time, but said nothing. They never took their eyes off Joel.

'I hope you're hungry,' said Jenny. 'We'll be eating shortly.'

Joel said he was looking forward to that.

'There's one thing I've often wondered about,' she said. 'Who did the cooking for you and Samuel? I ask because I know Samuel is hopeless when it comes to preparing food. At least, he was in those days.'

'Oh, it varied,' said Joel tentatively.

'Maybe Samuel has a girlfriend?'

'Occasionally.'

Joel had no desire to go any deeper into that question. Least of all did he want to tell her that he'd been his own mum all those years since she'd left them. And how angry he'd sometimes been at the mother who'd run away.

They had dinner in the kitchen. Joel sat at one short end of the table, opposite Jenny. The two sisters were still shy. Joel tried to think of something to say. But most of the time he was thinking about Samuel, who was by now lying on a bench in a train compartment, resting his head on his suitcase.

He hadn't packed any food to take with him for the journey.

He'd be hungry all the time until he got home. Even if there was a restaurant car on the train, it was bound to be far too expensive.

Joel had to acknowledge that he had a bad conscience. He shouldn't have accepted the money. At the very least he ought to have thought of buying something for Samuel to eat on the train.

Jenny had lots of questions to ask. And Joel answered them all. About how things had gone at school. And why he wanted to become a sailor like Samuel. Joel answered very tersely. He felt under pressure. Already he was thinking about finding a job on a ship as soon as possible.

It was beginning to get late.

The girls started getting ready for bed. Joel thought they were making a terrible din in the bathroom. But Jenny didn't seem to hear anything. Joel sat in the living room while they prepared for the coming night. Then Jenny came to ask him if he would like to accompany her to the girls' room and say good night.

He didn't want to; but he did even so.

'I expect you're probably tired,' said Jenny when all was quiet in the sisters' room.

Joel wasn't the least bit sleepy, but he wanted to be left in peace. After all those years without a mum, it was a bit much to suddenly find her hanging around all the time.

'Yes,' he said. 'I think I'll go to bed.'

'When you wake up tomorrow I'll probably have left already.'

She gave him a front door key.

'The girls are with a neighbour when I'm at work. So you don't need to worry about them.'

That was a big relief. The mere thought of having to be with them for a whole day was enough to make him want to run away.

'What are you going to do tomorrow? Will you be able to find your way round Stockholm?'

'I have a map. I'll manage OK.'

He had snuggled down into bed and was just about to switch off the light when she knocked on the door and came in.

'There's so much I want to know,' she said. 'And no doubt there's lots you want to know about me. We'll have to give it time.'

Joel mumbled something inaudible. He wanted her to leave. He couldn't cope with any more now.

She said good night and left the room.

The whole flat was soon silent.

Joel lay thinking about Samuel.

He missed the snoring that had always come rumbling into his bedroom through the walls.

Joel was on his own now. Although he had Jenny Rydén and two little sisters not far away.

But it was Samuel who wasn't there. That was what really mattered.

When he woke up next morning, the flat was quiet and empty. Outside, it was overcast but not raining. Joel had breakfast and changed into some clean underwear.

Then he went out.

When he came to the Seamen's Employment Exchange, the waiting room was full of people. All of them were seamen. They included a few boys who couldn't have been any older than he was himself. That worried him a bit. Perhaps all the boats were fully manned by now? Perhaps there wouldn't be a job for him?

When it was his turn he went to the desk and asked if his seaman's discharge book was ready yet.

It was!

It was dark blue. And had his name printed on the front. He felt as if he were already standing on deck. He could feel the floor swaying under his feet. He felt so happy.

He was forced to sit down so as not to lose his balance.

'Your first time?' somebody asked.

'Yes,' said Joel.

The one who asked had a freckled face and bright ginger hair.

'They'll be calling up soon now,' he said.

Joel didn't understand what he meant. Who would be calling up? Calling up what? But he didn't ask.

The explanation came almost immediately.

A hatch in the wall opened. A man with a sweaty face waved a few sheets of paper in the air.

'Electricians for *Neptun*. A bosun, an engineer. The engineer must be experienced. A steward for *Lindfjord*. And a deck hand. That's all for today. We'll be calling up again at ten tomorrow morning.'

Some of those waiting stood up and went to the desk. Others muttered in disgust and headed for the door. Joel understood what happened now. He would be back the next day at ten o'clock.

He could be a deck hand. Or a steward.

His excitement was tangible.

The man with the sweaty face was holding the whole world in his hands.

The waiting room slowly emptied. Joel stayed behind. He leafed through some of the magazines lying on a table. There were adverts for various shipping lines. What a lot of ships! Carrying cargoes of coal and iron ore, bananas and oil.

He was just about to leave when the hatch opened again. The man with the sweaty face stuck his head out and looked round. He was just about to close it again when he caught sight of Joel.

'What job are you looking for?' he shouted.

'I want to be a sailor,' said Joel.

'That's the daftest thing I've ever heard. Why else would you be sitting here?'

The man waved a sheet of paper at Joel.

'There was one more job going,' he said. 'The paper had fallen on the floor. The *MS Alta* is looking for a mess steward.'

Joel held his breath. Thoughts were racing through his head. A mess steward only went on deck in order to empty rubbish bins. He served meals in the mess, did the washing up, made beds and cleaned out cabins. Like a chambermaid in a hotel.

'I assume you're not interested,' said the man, and started to close the hatch.

'I'll take it,' Joel shouted.

The next moment he was standing by the hatch and produced his discharge book.

'She'll be docking at Värtahamnen tonight. Be there tomorrow morning at eight o'clock. Ask for the chief steward.'

'Who?'

The man behind the hatch opened Joel's discharge book and nodded.

'Your first voyage, I see. Go on board and ask for the chief steward. His name's Pirinen. He's a Finn. But he speaks Swedish. Go and see him. If he likes the look of you, you come back here and sign on. Is that clear?'

Joel nodded.

He was handed the sheet of paper, and the hatch closed.

Everything had happened so quickly that he'd hardly been able to keep up.

First he'd been given his seaman's discharge book. And then he'd got a posting the very first day.

What kind of a ship was it, this *MS Alta*?

Joel hesitated. Then he knocked on the hatch. It opened immediately.

The man was wiping the sweat from his face with a piece of newspaper.

'Are you still here?'

'I just wanted to know what kind of a boat it was.'

'Grängesberg line.'

'Where's it sailing to?'

The man behind the hatch sighed deeply.

'How the hell do I know? But it's an iron ore freighter. So it'll be going to a port where it can load up with iron ore. And then it will sail to another one where it can unload.'

Liberia, Joel thought. Africa.

He remembered what Geegee had said.

So it was the same shipping line as the *MS Karmas*.

'Anything more you want to know? We're about to close now.'

'No,' said Joel. 'Nothing else.'

The hatch closed once more.

Joel went out into the street.

His first thought was to tell Samuel about it. But that was impossible. He was still on a train somewhere on his way north.

Joel felt extremely excited.

All the ships he'd ever dreamt about had faded away.

Now there was a real one. A ship called the *MS Alta*, at this very moment heading for Stockholm.

Joel set off walking. Slowly at first, then faster and faster.

On the way to Östgötagatan he bought a picture postcard and a stamp. When he came to Jenny's flat he found a pen and sat down at the kitchen table.

He wrote to Samuel.

I got my seaman's discharge book today. And I've got a job. On a ship called the MS Alta. I'm off to sea now. See you on Pitcairn Island.

Greetings, Joel

He wasn't sure about the last sentence.
See you on Pitcairn Island.
Maybe Samuel would think he was being provoked? But he left it anyway. They'd talked about that so many times, after all. Sat poring over sea charts and looking for the little dot in the middle of the Pacific Ocean. Where Fletcher and his men had gone into hiding after their mutiny against that cruel Captain Bligh.

That's what he'd written. It could stay as it was.
He ran down the stairs and into the street, and soon found a postbox. He read through what he'd written one more time. Then he popped the card into the box.

Jenny and his little sisters came back together. Joel was lying on his bed in the little room behind the kitchen, and heard their voices. He went to the living room and greeted them. Then he told them what had happened.

'I'll be signing on tomorrow. I'm afraid I won't be able to stay any longer.'

Jenny sat down on a chair. She seemed disappointed.

'So you're leaving already?'

'Yes.'

'Where are you sailing to?'

'Africa. Liberia.'

'As far away as Africa?'

'Or Oxelösund. Nothing is certain. It depends where the cargoes are. And where they have to be taken to.'

'You must know if you're going to Africa or Oxelösund, surely?'

'I'll probably be going to both places. And Belgium as well.'

Jenny shook her head. Then she burst out laughing.

'You're just like Samuel. He was always going to either Rio de Janeiro or London. And I never knew where he'd come from.'

'You know how it is, then,' said Joel.

The two sisters stood and listened but said nothing. They gaped wide-eyed at their big brother.

'If it is Africa, I'll bring a present back for you,' said Joel. 'A monkey skin or something like that.'

'Good Lord, no!' said Jenny. 'I wouldn't want that. Not a monkey skin. Anything at all but that.'

That evening Jenny and Joel sat up for ages, talking. Time had turned out to be so short. But when Joel finally went to bed and switched off the light, he could hardly remember anything they'd said.

All he could think about was the next day.

I'll have time to think about Jenny later, he told himself.

I've found her now. That's the main thing. And I've got two little sisters – who kick up a hell of a row in the bathroom.

But what all that means is something I can think about later.

The first thing I have to do is to walk up the gangway onto the ship that at this very moment is on its way to Stockholm to pick me up.

And the next day, shortly before eight o'clock, Joel got off the tram and saw the ship that had berthed during the night. *MS Alta* was bigger than *MS Karmas*. The hatches were just being opened. Joel could feel his heart pounding. Then he went through the dock gates and approached the gangway. The side of the ship towered above him like a mountain. He went on board.

A sailor wearing overalls came towards him. He gave Joel a friendly smile.

'Are you going to sign on?'

'Yes.'

'Deck or mess?'

'I'm going to be a mess steward.'

'Our new Kalle, then. He was good, the one we had before you. Apart from the washing up – he wasn't much good at that.'

The man looked Joel in the eye.

'Can you wash up?' he asked.

161

'Yes,' said Joel. 'That's about all I can do.'

The man pointed towards the stern of the ship.

'Pirinen will no doubt be back there, drinking coffee with the cook. I assume he's the one you have to see.'

Joel walked slowly in the direction the man had indicated. He was so high up above the water.

He took a deep breath. As if to convince himself that what he was doing was true.

Then he went to meet Pirinen. And was duly approved and signed on. That very same day he moved into his cabin.

Jenny wanted to take the girls with her and have a look at the ship. But Joel said no.

If it had been Samuel, that would have been different.

He started work the following day. He was disappointed to discover that the ship would be staying in Stockholm for a whole week. Nobody knew which would be their next port. Somebody said Narvik. Somebody else said England. But nobody knew. It would be some days before they found out.

And Joel worked. He laid tables and washed up, cleaned and made beds. He got to know the ship and the people working on it. And every night he collapsed into bed exhausted.

They eventually discovered where they would be sailing to. Joel was disappointed. Their destination would be Luleå.

The far north of Sweden, he thought. Even further

north than the place where Samuel and I have been living all those years.

Nevertheless, he was on his way at last.

He was woken up at four in the morning by the vibrations from the engines. He could hear the mooring ropes being cast off. Then the propeller rumbled into action.

The journey had begun.

12

In Luleå Joel bought a notebook with a black cover.

That same day he started his logbook. His first entry was dated June 17.

Arrived Luleå.
Perhaps it was good that my first voyage brought
me here.
You can't get any further north.
Now I have to sail south.
Luleå. June 17, 1959. 8.35 p.m.

He'd made up his mind to write something every day. It didn't need to be much. But there would have to be at least one word, a date and a time.

He also posted two letters in Luleå.

The first was to Samuel. He explained how he'd collected his discharge book and the very same day signed on with his first ship. He described the vessel, how it was 20,000 tons, and that he was currently in Luleå.

He hoped that Samuel's journey home had gone well.

He promised to write from his next port of call, and included the unused half of his train ticket in the envelope.

If Samuel wanted to write back, he knew what he needed to do. The letter should be addressed to the shipping line.

The other letter was to Jenny Rydén.

That was more difficult to write. He tore up several attempts. In the end he didn't have the strength to write any more, and so his latest effort would just have to do.

He asked her to hang the photograph of Samuel up again. Assuming he was right in thinking she'd taken it down. If she didn't do that, he would never visit her again.

But he gave her an alternative. If she didn't want to have Samuel on her wall, instead she could remove the picture of the man with the close-cropped hair. Then there would be two marks on the wallpaper.

He wondered how she would react. She might be angry? Perhaps she wouldn't want to see him ever again? Well, he'd just have to take that risk.

And so Joel's life at sea got under way.

The ship sailed from Luleå to Middlesbrough. They docked at first light. Joel was standing on deck, gazing at this foreign country swathed in mist. It was the first time he'd ever been outside Swedish territory. They'd had fine weather all the way. The North Sea had been dead calm.

That evening, Joel went ashore with a deck hand by the name of Frans, who was from Gotland. Frans had been a sailor for two years already, and had been to Middlesbrough before. He knew the dockland district. Joel drank two pints of beer in a pub, and got a splitting headache. By the time they had to go back to their ship, Joel had fallen asleep over the table. The following day, when he was woken up at six o'clock, he was sick.

He'd got used to the work by now. The days were humdrum. First of all he had his own breakfast. Then he set the tables and served 24 covers in the mess where the ordinary sailors used to eat. There were two other messes. But the one where the captain, the mate and the chief engineer ate was called the wardroom, and the steward there was called a wardroom steward. After breakfast, Joel's work was to wash up and then clean out the cabins. He had a few hours' free time in the afternoons, and then worked again until eight in the evening.

He had a cabin of his own. That had surprised him. In the days when he'd dreamt about becoming a sailor, he thought everybody slept together in a big dormitory. He realised that a lot of what Samuel used to talk about no longer applied in modern times.

His cabin wasn't very big. It had a bunk fixed to the wall, a washbasin, a wardrobe and a chair. And a porthole.

It seemed to him that he'd never had better living quarters in the whole of his life. The engines throbbing away deep down inside the ship rocked him to sleep.

They stayed in Middlesbrough for a whole week. On Saturday Joel accompanied several of the other crew members to a nearby city called Sunderland, where they watched a football match.

Every day was different.

Something new was happening all the time.

*

166

They left Middlesbrough and headed for Narvik. Northwards again. But Joel had decided to be patient. This was his first ship after all. An iron ore trader. He would begin by getting used to life at sea. Then he would apply for work on other types of boat. He had plenty of time.

The second night on the North Sea, Joel was woken up by being tossed around in his bunk. A wind had blown up. He could feel his stomach reacting already. But he forced himself to go back to sleep. It would have blown over by morning.

But in fact it was gale force winds when he woke up. When he staggered out of bed, he had to cling on to the wardrobe door so as not to fall over.

The rest of the day was a nightmare. Joel alternated work with throwing up, had to watch plates of food falling onto the floor and sliding around, and he began to wonder why on earth he'd ever wanted to go to sea. Samuel had talked about being seasick. But this was something far worse than he'd ever imagined. He spoke to the cook, whose name was Axelsson and who was holding on to the stove to remain upright while he was frying the potatoes, and asked how long it was going to go on like this.

'Oh, it'll last all the way to Narvik. But it'll blow over eventually.'

Joel stared at the potatoes sizzling away in the fat – and only just managed to get to the nearest toilet before throwing up again.

That evening he was so tired that he collapsed into bed without even bothering to get undressed. He was dreading the next morning.

Joel was seasick until they were well into the fjord at Narvik. Then, at long last, he could feel it ebbing away.

He was never seasick again.

He was one of the lucky ones who had the ability to get used to it. But Frans had stories about a bosun he knew who'd suffered from seasickness for over forty years.

The weeks passed by.

Joel found himself in Narvik four times. And then Bristol, Middlesbrough again, Ghent, and eventually Holland. A port close to Amsterdam.

Frans had been to Amsterdam before. One evening he told Joel a series of stories that Joel suspected were made up. About women sitting in windows and offering themselves for sale. A whole district full of women sitting in windows. Joel refused to believe that it was true.

'You go there and see for yourself,' Frans said.

Joel made up his mind to do just that. When they came to Holland, Pirinen gave Joel a day off. So he went to the telegraphist's office and cashed in 200 kronor of his wages. This was the first time he'd taken out money. He'd never had so much money in his hand before.

The intention had been that Frans would go with him to Amsterdam. But Frans wasn't allowed shore leave as there was some essential work to be done that needed his presence. So Joel had to travel alone.

He'd decided that now was when it was going to happen.

He'd written in his logbook:

We're sailing through the Kiel Canal. It's high time
I took the step from Sonja Mattsson to something
more. August 22, 1959. 7.44 p.m.

Joel took the train.

Frans had told him that the women who sat in the windows were in a district close to the Amsterdam central railway station.

When he got there, he consulted a timetable in order to establish when the last train left for the harbour where his ship was berthed.

Then he stepped out into Amsterdam. He was nervous. He didn't know what was in store. Frans had tried to explain it to him. He ought to walk around, have a good look at all the windows, and choose a woman he fancied. Then they'd let him into a room at the back of the house. He'd have to pay first. Frans had kept stressing how important that was, over and over again. First the money. Otherwise he might find himself confronted by some frightening character who'd been sitting in another back room, listening to the radio.

First the money, Joel thought. He had it in his pocket. The telegraphist had paid him in Dutch guilders.

Joel hadn't a clue about what would happen next. He was worried that he wouldn't be able to cope. And he wasn't at all sure what it was that he'd be expected to cope with. She might throw him out if he did it wrong.

But obviously, he hadn't mentioned to Frans that this would be his first time. Or that he was worried.

He had a suspicion that it would be easier if he'd had something to drink. Not too much. Just enough to banish his nerves. So he went to a bar next to the station. He had a beer. Only one. His body felt warmer already. When he left the bar, he found his way to the red light district. There were a lot of people in the streets. Lots of sailors, just like him.

And then there were all the women.

Frans hadn't exaggerated.

They were sitting on chairs in brightly lit windows, with fixed expressions on their faces. Just like tailors' dummies.

Joel felt both nervous and sexually excited. He hardly dared look at the women. Most of them were half naked and heavily made up. Some were smoking. Joel paused at a window where lots of other men were already standing, and took a good look. He could hide in the background there.

Then he went to a bar and ordered a whisky. Frans drank whisky. Nothing else. Joel forced it down him.

Samuel would have swallowed it in a single gulp, Joel thought. No doubt Samuel has also been to this very same place.

Who would he have chosen?

Joel decided to drink another whisky. That would have to be enough.

He paid and left. Now he felt bold enough to stand in front of a window all by himself.

But how would he be able to choose?

He wished there had been a girl who looked like Sonja

Mattsson. But he couldn't see one. He moved on. The lit-up windows came to an end. He was just going to retrace his steps when somebody spoke to him from out of the shadows. He couldn't see who it was at first. Then a woman appeared in front of him. She hadn't come from one of the brightly lit windows, but Joel had no doubt she was one of the same type. For sale. She spoke English. Said how much it cost, and pointed into the shadows. Joel could just make out the outline of a door.

She couldn't have been more than twenty-five. Like Sonja Mattsson. She had brown hair and wasn't as heavily made up as the women Joel had seen in the windows.

She took hold of his arm.

Joel thought he ought to make a run for it.

But instead he accompanied her into the shadows.

There was a steep staircase behind the door. She ushered him up it, in front of her.

What the hell am I doing in here? Joel thought.

They came to a room where there was a bed with a red cover. A radio could be heard in a neighbouring room.

She sat down on the bed and stretched out her hand.

He gave her the money she'd asked for.

Then she started to unbutton his trousers.

Then she took off her own green trousers. Joel just had time to see that she was wearing nothing underneath before she pulled him down on top of her on the bed. She hadn't removed the cover.

He wasn't at all sure what happened next. He was aroused now. Felt how he penetrated her, and then it was all over almost before it had started.

It all happened so quickly, he was rather confused. She pulled him up off the bed, gave him a tissue to wipe himself with, and urged him to take care when he went down the stairs.

'Be careful,' she said. 'Be careful.'

Then she vanished into the room where the radio was on.

Joel pulled up his trousers and stumbled out onto the staircase.

Once he was out in the street again, he asked himself what had happened. It was nothing like he'd imagined it would be.

Even so, he knew exactly what he was going to write in his logbook.

Amsterdam.
Done it at last.
August 24, 1959. 10.10 p.m.

He went back to the railway station and found the right platform. Shortly before midnight he found himself walking up the gangway again.

Frans was standing by the rail, smoking.

'Well,' he said. 'How did it go?'

'Good,' said Joel. 'Bloody good.'

Then he went to his cabin before Frans had time to ask any more questions. But he could hear Frans chuckling to himself by the ship's rail.

The days passed. Joel was still waiting for a message:

next destination, Liberia. But it was still Narvik and Bristol and Ghent. In the middle of September they also undertook a voyage from Narvik to Luleå. It took fourteen days. Joel began to lose faith. By the end of November he began to wonder if he ought to sign off this ship and try one from another shipping line. One that didn't only fill its holds with iron ore.

All this time Joel had only received one letter from Samuel. It had arrived at the end of October. Samuel wrote that all was well, but not much more than that. Joel had a suspicion that things weren't as good as Samuel claimed. How was he managing on his own? Who was cooking for him? Had he remembered to put cold water in the dirty porridge pan?

What worried Joel most of all was if Samuel was drinking heavily. Who was keeping an eye on him when Joel wasn't around?

Joel had almost made up his mind to sign off. But then came the message he'd been waiting for: the next voyage would be to Liberia. They would be there for Christmas. Joel didn't hesitate for a moment. This was what he'd been waiting for. Once he'd been to Africa, he would sign off and pay a visit to Samuel.

He wrote to both Samuel and Jenny. She had written him several letters, but she'd never referred to Joel's request that the photograph of Samuel should go back up on the wall. Or that the man with the close-cropped hair should be taken down.

Joel had never referred to that again. Soon enough he

would be able to see with his own eyes what had happened, if anything.

He wrote about the forthcoming voyage.

The journey to Liberia.

The journey to the end of the world.

Joel arrived in Africa the day before Christmas Eve, 1959. The African coast could be seen like an enticing mirage on the port side of the ship. Every morning when Joel woke up, it was warmer than the day before. And the sea changed colour. It became lighter. The blue gradually turned into green. He saw dolphins and flying fish. Every evening he stood at the stern of the ship and looked up at the starry sky.

On December 20 he wrote in his logbook:

I sometimes think about that dog. The one I thought I saw that time. On its way to a star. But I was only a child then. I didn't know any better. Here everything is just as bright and sparkling as it is at home in mid-winter. December 20. Just south of the Cape Verde Islands. 10.22 p.m.

They stayed in Liberia for four days.

Joel went ashore whenever he was free. He wandered around in the teeming mass of people, breathed in all the unusual smells, and was fascinated by the beautiful women carrying extremely heavy burdens on their heads. He bought some shells for his little sisters, a colourful loincloth for Jenny and a drum for Samuel. On Christmas Eve he wrote in his logbook:

Liberia.
I know now that I've done the right thing. A sailor
is what I'm going to be. On my next ship I'll be a
deck hand. One day I might start to study in order
to become a bosun. After Christmas, I'll go home
and collect Samuel. He's forgotten what it was like.
I shall remind him. December 24, 1959.

While they were berthed in Liberia, Joel also fell in love.

Every time he went ashore, a young girl came up to him and asked if he needed anybody to wash his clothes. He said no. But she was persistent and came back every day. Her name was Milena. And she was sixteen years old.

They used to speak on the quay. Always the same thing. But Joel thought she reminded him of Sonja Mattsson, despite the fact that she was very black.

The day before New Year's Eve they weighed anchor and headed north. Milena stood on the quay, waving. Joel had given her some money as he'd realised she was very poor.

Pirinen was standing beside him at the rail, smoking.

'When will we be coming back here?' Joel asked.

Pirinen grinned. He'd seen Joel waving, and Milena waving back.

'Never,' said Pirinen. 'Forget her.'

But Joel had no intention of forgetting Milena. And he knew that what Pirinen had said wasn't true. Pirinen could be annoying at times. But Joel had learnt how to deal with that.

Their next port of call after Liberia was Narvik. Joel had decided to sign off at the end of January. By then he would have saved nearly a thousand kronor. It was time to pay Samuel a visit.

But when they got to Narvik, and the heat of Africa had become a distant memory, he found a letter waiting for him. The telegraphist gave it to Joel just after he'd finished washing up after breakfast. It was from Samuel. Joel recognised the spidery handwriting.

He went to his cabin, lay down on his bed and opened the letter.

It was very short. Not many words. But Joel would never forget them.

Joel,
I hope all is going well for you on the Alta. I hope the trip to Africa was a great experience. I think it would be best if you came home now. You'll remember that I had stomach pains last summer. They've become worse now. It's not possible to say what will happen. So perhaps it would be best if you came home.

Samuel

Joel felt as if he'd been punched in the stomach.

So Samuel was ill.

He recalled what he'd thought at the hotel, when Samuel came back from the hospital.

Samuel might die.

He started to panic. He would have to go to Samuel straight away. He couldn't put it off. But he couldn't just abandon ship and leave his work just like that. There were rules about how much notice you had to give before handing in your discharge book and asking to sign off.

I need to speak to somebody, he thought. Pirinen? He wouldn't understand. The telegraphist? He wouldn't be able to do anything.

Joel got up from his bunk. He would speak to the captain. Captain Håkansson.

He was often gruff and angry, but that couldn't be helped. Joel left his bunk and walked up the stairs to the bridge. If the captain wasn't ashore, he'd be bound to be in his cabin.

Joel knocked on the door.

'Come in.'

Joel opened the door. Captain Håkansson was sitting at a desk, writing. He frowned.

'I'm busy,' he said.

Joel could feel that he was in danger of bursting into tears.

'It's my father,' he said. 'He's very ill.'

Joel held out the letter. Captain Håkansson beckoned to him.

Then he stared hard at Joel, who could feel the tears in his eyes.

'I don't want to read a private letter you have received,' said the captain, 'but I can see from your face that it's true.'

'I have to go home,' said Joel.

The captain nodded.

'I'll fix it,' he said curtly.

He stood up.

'I'll have a word with the chief steward and the telegraphist. Prepare to leave by this evening.'

'Thank you,' said Joel.

'I've had good reports about you,' said the captain. 'You do your job well. Never any problems.'

He nodded towards the door. The conversation was over.

That same evening Joel boarded the night train to Sweden.

13

It was late when Joel got off the train that winter evening.

And it was very cold. The thermometer hanging on the station wall showed minus 31 degrees Celsius. Joel pulled his scarf over his mouth and nose. He was the only one to leave the train. The stationmaster waved his flag and withdrew to the warmth of the staff rooms.

Joel was all alone. He had bought a sailor's kitbag in Narvik. Inside it were his clothes and the presents he'd bought in Liberia.

He set off walking. He took the old road by the river.

He didn't know how many times he'd walked or cycled along that road. But now it felt like the first time ever.

He was in a hurry. During the long journey from Narvik he had felt his unease growing all the way. He must have read the letter from Samuel at least a hundred times. In order to grasp what it meant. He'd tried to convince himself that Samuel was drunk when he wrote the letter. Drunk and lonely, in a kitchen full of burnt saucepans. Joel had to go home now in order to clean up and wash the dishes.

But Samuel would never write a letter after being out drinking. So Joel tried to convince himself his father was exaggerating. That might be a possibility. Samuel sometimes imagined that he was more ill than he really was.

But deep down, Joel knew. He'd known even in the hotel in Stockholm, the moment Samuel came in through the door.

Samuel was so ill that he might die.

Joel walked as fast as he could. The cold air was scratching at his lungs.

He suddenly stopped in his tracks.

What if Samuel was dead already? Or was in hospital?

He set off again even more quickly. He was on the hill now. He'd soon be able to see the house. See if there was a light on in the kitchen.

The road was deserted. Snow was piled high on both sides.

There was nobody else about.

Another twenty metres and he'd be able to see the house. He increased speed even more, despite the fact that he really wanted to stop.

But now he could see the house. And there was a light on in the kitchen.

So Samuel wasn't dead. And he wasn't in hospital.

He was at home.

Joel slowed down. He needed to prepare himself now. What was in store for him? What would Samuel say when Joel suddenly appeared in the doorway, stamping the snow off his boots? Joel hadn't been able to inform Samuel that he'd be arriving that very evening.

He went through the gate and into the garden. Past where he'd slept in an old bed one night a year ago. When he'd resolved to live to be a hundred, and had started to toughen himself up. He shook his head. He'd never do anything like that again. He opened the door and listened. As he did so it occurred to him that he ought to have knocked. Samuel wasn't expecting visitors. He might think it was a burglar.

He went into the kitchen. The door of Samuel's room was half open. The radio was silent. But the light was on.

He put his kitbag on the floor. The sink was empty, he noticed. No sign of any burnt saucepans. Or empty bottles.

He took off his woolly hat and mittens, and approached the door.

Samuel was in bed.

He was awake, and looked at Joel.

He smiled.

'So you've come?' he said. 'I thought you would. But I didn't know when.'

'I came as soon as I got your letter,' said Joel.

There were bottles of medicine on the bedside table. And Samuel was pale. Unshaven and pale. Although he was under the bedclothes, Joel could see that his dad had lost weight. He hasn't been eating enough, Joel thought. Perhaps he hasn't been eating properly since he got back home.

Pools of water started to form round Joel's boots.

'I'll just take my boots off,' he said, and went to the kitchen. He pulled out his usual chair. It scraped against the floor. He recognised the sound.

When he'd taken off his boots and jacket he went back to Samuel's room. He sat down on the edge of the bed.

'You're growing bigger and bigger,' said Samuel.

'I'm five foot eleven now,' said Joel.

'That's taller than I am.'

Silence.

'I got your letter,' said Joel.

Samuel pulled a face.

'I had to write it,' he said. 'But we don't need to discuss that now. How long do you intend staying?'

'I don't know.'

'We can talk about that tomorrow.'

He always wants to put everything off, Joel thought. Samuel Gustafson has never come straight to the point. The whole of his life has been an elaborate detour.

'I'm not really sure if there's any food in,' said Samuel apologetically. 'In case you're hungry.'

'I'm not hungry.'

'You can take a look in the pantry.'

'I'm not hungry.'

'But I've made your bed. As I knew you'd come to see me.'

That was an important piece of information, Joel thought.

It means he's not so ill that he can't stand on his own two legs.

'I got your letter,' he said again.

'I had to write it.'

We can sit here like this all night, Joel thought, saying the same things over and over again. I ask and he answers, and we get nowhere.

'We can wait until tomorrow,' said Samuel. 'You must be tired.'

'We can't wait until tomorrow at all. I want to know how you are.'

Samuel nodded.

Joel waited.

'You remember last summer,' Samuel began.

'I remember.'

'At the hotel. How I had stomach pains. And then all that hospital business.'

'They were going to send you a letter.'

Samuel paused again.

Joel was so frightened that he was trembling.

They were nearly there now. The reason why Samuel had written that letter.

'They sent me a letter,' he said slowly, as if every word was the result of a big effort.

'What did it say?'

'That things weren't all that good. The tests they'd done. They said I should go to the hospital here and show them the letter. So I did. I showed it to one of the top doctors. He said I had cancer. In my liver. And that it was incurable.'

There was a thudding in Joel's head. Samuel was dying.

He wasn't trembling any more. He was completely calm.

'It was incurable,' Samuel said again. 'So now I'm here in bed. I can't go to work. I just lie here.'

Joel didn't know what to say.

'Who does your food shopping for you?' he asked in the end.

'Sara's arranged for somebody to buy me the basic

necessities. And a nurse comes to see me every other day. But I'll probably have to go into hospital soon.'

'Are you in pain?'

'Not much. Not like it was in Stockholm.'

He produced one of his skinny hands from under the covers and pointed at all the tubes and bottles.

'They've given me some excellent medicine. That sorts everything out.'

'But you said it was incurable?'

'I mean it deals with the pain.'

'What else did they say?'

'There wasn't much more they could say. If it's incurable, that's that.'

'Are you going to die?'

Joel wished he could have eaten his words.

But strangely enough, Samuel only laughed.

'I'm not going to die,' he said. 'Not while you're here at home, at least. You can still go on living even if you've got something incurable. I actually think I've been feeling better these last few days. It might go away, even if it is incurable.'

'Yes,' said Joel.

'For God's sake,' said Samuel. 'People go on living even if they have no arms or legs. It would be a poor show if I couldn't go on living without a liver. Don't you think?'

Was that a real question? Or was Samuel convinced that he was right? Joel didn't know.

And so he merely nodded.

He agreed. With whatever it was that Samuel thought.

Samuel was trying to raise himself into a sitting position.

'There must be something to eat,' he said.

'I'm not hungry.'

'But you must want a cup of coffee, eh? And then I want to hear all about what you've been doing.'

'That can wait until tomorrow.'

Samuel sank back into the pillows.

'You're right,' he said. 'That can wait. I'm a bit tired.'

'Can I get you anything?'

Samuel looked at his glass.

'A drop of water. That's all.'

Joel took the glass to the kitchen. Perhaps it's possible to live without a liver. Joel didn't understand why you needed a liver. And where was it? In the stomach somewhere?

When he'd given Samuel his glass of water, he went back to the kitchen and unpacked the drum. It was quite small. The skin was brown, and the drum was a hollowed out piece of tree trunk.

Samuel put on his glasses and examined it carefully.

'It's terrific,' he said.

He tentatively tapped his fingers on the skin.

'Sounds good,' he said. 'A real drum.'

Joel wondered why he'd bought it. Why on earth had he bought Samuel a drum? Couldn't he have thought of something better?

'Perhaps I can learn to play it,' said Samuel. 'Become a drummer in my old age.'

'I'd thought of buying you a monkey skin,' said Joel. 'But I didn't get much time on shore leave.'

'A drum's fine,' said Samuel. 'I've always wanted a real African drum.'

Joel knew that wasn't true. It was just Samuel's way of saying thank you.

Joel put the drum on the floor.

'I want to know everything tomorrow,' said Samuel. 'But I think I'd better go to sleep now. All this medicine makes me sleepy.'

'We'll talk tomorrow,' said Joel.

'I lie here thinking,' said Samuel. 'When I can't sleep, it's as if the house were a ship. And I can hear the anchor being lifted, and the house sails out of the harbour.'

He shook his head.

'Funny how childish you can get sometimes.'

Joel stood up.

'I hope you can get some sleep.'

'I'm glad you've come. We can talk more tomorrow.'

'Yes, we can talk tomorrow.'

Joel went to his room.

Everything was still there. The bed, the table, the chair, the alarm clock, the roller blind. Just the same as when he'd left it. It felt as if that was a long time ago. He lay down on top of the bed. There was a creaking and knocking in the wall beside his head. The cold was singing in the wooden beams behind the wallpaper.

Joel tried to understand the situation. Samuel was incurably ill. But he thought he might be able to go on living even so. He didn't seem to be afraid. If you're going to die, surely that must instil fear? Joel couldn't imagine any other possibility.

He listened for Samuel's snores. But everything was totally silent.

So Samuel has had the same dream as I had, Joel thought. He's dreamt that the house was a ship. That casts off and floats down the river towards the sea. This flat is the bridge. Captain Samuel Gustafson. First Mate Joel Gustafson. A father and son who can steer the ship through the worst hurricanes imaginable.

That was a remarkable thought for Joel. That he and Samuel had experienced the same dreams. They'd both transformed this ramshackle, rickety old house into a ship.

Joel got up and tiptoed into the kitchen. Samuel had switched off the light. The door was ajar, just as Joel had left it. Samuel still hadn't started snoring. But Joel could hear that he was asleep. His breathing in the darkness of his room was deep and heavy.

Joel crept up onto the window seat. It was barely big enough to hold him now. A streetlight illuminated the deserted road. It was minus 32 degrees now. Midwinter. Joel shuddered. And thought about Liberia. And the girl who had waved to him.

Before he knew where he was, he had fallen asleep. When he was woken up by cramp in his leg, he had no idea where he was. Then the penny dropped. And he could hear Samuel snoring.

I must find out if you can go on living with a liver

that's incurably damaged, Joel thought. That's the very first thing I need to do.

Joel woke up the next morning and heard Samuel clattering away in the kitchen. He investigated and found Samuel making porridge. But he hadn't got dressed. He was wearing his old dressing gown over his pyjamas.

'Cold water in the pan,' he said with a smile.

Joel couldn't believe that Samuel had a life-threatening illness. Perhaps it was incurable. But was it life-threatening?

When they'd finished breakfast Samuel wanted to talk about what Joel had experienced during his first months as a sailor.

'I'll tell you all about that later,' said Joel. 'I have a few things I must see to first.'

It was still very cold when he left the house. He set off up the hill to the hospital. There were several people about now. But he didn't see them. He burrowed his chin down into his jacket, and walked as fast as he could. But after a while, he paused. Why was he going to the hospital? There were easier ways of finding out what a liver was. He turned round and started retracing his steps.

He didn't stop until he'd come to the slaughterhouse, on the very edge of the town. He'd worked there as an errand boy the previous summer. He knew the boss and several of the slaughtermen. He stamped his feet to shake off the snow and went into the office. The boss was called Herbert Lundgren, and had a freckled face despite the fact that he was nearly sixty. He was wearing a white coat and a peaked cap.

'Joel?' he said. 'I heard you'd gone to sea?'

'So I have. I'm just visiting.'

Lundgren frowned.

'I heard that Samuel was ill. How is he?'

'He's fine. But that's why I've come. I want to know what a liver is.'

'A liver?'

'Yes. Where it is, and what it does.'

'Why do you want to know that?'

'Samuel's liver is damaged beyond repair.'

Lundgren said nothing.

'But Samuel thinks he can carry on living even so.'

'Maybe he can,' said Lundgren slowly. 'I'm not a doctor. I don't really know about such things.'

'Where is your liver?'

Lundgren pointed to the side of his stomach.

'That's all I wanted to know.'

Joel put his woolly hat back on, and started wrapping his scarf round his face.

'There's one thing you ought to be clear about,' said Lundgren.

Joel looked at him.

'What's that?'

'Oh, nothing. Nothing at all.'

Joel left the slaughterhouse. It was getting light now. The sun was just beginning to rise above the fir-covered hills that surrounded the little town. He wondered what Herbert Lundgren had been going to say. But Samuel will no doubt pull through, he thought. It takes more than this to knock out an old sailor like Samuel Gustafson.

He went to Ehnström's grocery store and bought a few things. It was Mrs Ehnström who served him.

'Joel,' she said. 'I thought you were at sea?'

'I'm just visiting. Samuel is ill.'

'So we heard. Poor man.'

'He'll be all right. It's just something about his liver that's not as it should be.'

'No doubt he's drunk too much over the years. That's how it goes.'

Joel could feel himself getting angry. Samuel's drinking habits had nothing to do with Mrs Ehnström.

'It affects the liver.'

'Samuel feels better now,' said Joel angrily. 'Potatoes, please. And jam.'

His anger lasted all the way home. But when he got as far as the kitchen door, he heard some mysterious noises coming from inside. At first he couldn't understand what it was.

Then he realised.

Samuel was playing the drum. He was tapping his fingertips on the brown skin.

He's not going to die, Joel thought. A man who gets out of bed in the middle of winter in order to play an African drum can't possibly be so ill that he's going to die.

Joel coughed and stamped his feet to dislodge the snow. The noises from the kitchen ceased abruptly. Joel waited for a few seconds before opening the door.

Samuel was sitting in his usual place at the table.
He'd shaved. And he was smiling.

'I'm so glad you've come home,' he said. 'We've a lot to talk about. I feel much better already.'

That evening they took out the old sea charts again.

Joel had made the dinner and then done the washing up. Samuel didn't eat much. But he said he thought the food was very good.

They finished off the meal with a cup of coffee. And Joel talked about his travels. He said nothing about that evening in Amsterdam. But he did tell his dad about the girl who wanted to wash his clothes in Liberia.

At no time during the evening did Samuel ask about Jenny. Nor did Joel mention her. If Samuel didn't want to know, that was up to him.

It started to get late.

'I've been thinking,' said Samuel. 'I think it's time now. For me as well.'

Joel couldn't believe his ears. Had Samuel really made up his mind? Did he really have to be struck down by an incurable illness before realising that it was high time he put away his saws and axes?

'Are you serious?'

'I've never been more serious in all my life. As soon as I feel a bit better, I'll sign on again.'

'Maybe we can both work on the same ship?'

'Then it won't be long before we go ashore on Pitcairn Island.'

'How long will it take? Before you're better?'

'Not very long.'

'A month?'

'At most.'

'What about the incurable illness?'

'It doesn't show.'

Joel could still scarcely believe that it was true. It was as if he could hear a distant foghorn sounding inside his head. A foghorn warning all ships enveloped by the mist.

That feeling he'd had at the Raven Hotel. And the letter.

Samuel is so ill that he's going to die.

But Joel banished the thought.

Samuel really did seem to be better now than he'd been the night before.

It was turned midnight when Samuel went to bed. Joel stayed up a bit longer at the kitchen table, poring over the sea charts.

Then he went to bed as well.

The next day he'd start writing to other shipping lines.

A few hours later he was dragged out of his slumbers by an unfamiliar noise. He opened his eyes in the darkness and wondered what it was.

Then he froze stiff.

It was Samuel.

He was sitting in the kitchen, crying.

14

That night Samuel told Joel the full facts.

He would never be able to sign up on a ship again. The illness he was suffering from would never go away. Nor could he count on it getting any better. When Joel appeared in the doorway with his sailor's kitbag, Samuel had felt that despite everything, things could go back to normal. But when he woke up in the night, he couldn't indulge in make-believe any longer. He would never sail to Pitcairn Island. The only journey he would make in the rest of his life would be to the hospital.

Joel didn't feel afraid. He had gone along with Samuel's dream of everything turning out all right because that was easier than facing the difficult realities. Now he felt relieved. Knowing the facts.

Samuel was going to die. No matter how odd that seemed.

Joel felt helpless. And angry. It was unfair that Samuel had fallen ill. Why couldn't it have been somebody else instead? Everybody had a liver. Why should it be Samuel's that had gone wrong?

There was an invisible word that was never mentioned that night. Death. Neither of them wanted to say it. But they both knew what they were talking about even so.

'I try not to think about it,' said Samuel. 'So as not to

be frightened. It's true that I always make a mess of shaving, and I've done some silly things in my life. But nobody will be able to say that I'm afraid.'

During the night they also spoke about Jenny.

It happened out of the blue.

'I don't regret what I said to her. But there again, I'd like you to know that I can understand her. She was never suited to life up here in the forests. She was never suited to life with me. She thought I was different from the way I am. And the same applied to the person I thought she was. I know I'm not easy to live with. What with all my peculiar habits.'

Joel had made some more coffee. He gave Samuel a refill.

'But you know all about that, of course,' said Samuel. 'That I'm not so easy to live with.'

Joel said nothing. He had nothing to say.

'I think that you and Jenny can be good friends,' said Samuel. 'And nothing makes me more pleased than that.'

Samuel lifted his cup of coffee, but as he did so the pain came back. He grimaced with pain.

'I think I'd better go and lie down,' he said. 'You don't need to help me. I'll manage. And you need to get some sleep as well.'

Joel remained in the kitchen. He didn't even go to sit on the window seat. His head was empty. Various images were hopping around. Totally without context.

After a while he got up and trudged back to bed.

I'll never be able to sleep again for the rest of my life, he thought.

Then he fell asleep. With the covers over his head.

When he came to look back, Joel would recall Samuel's last days as the most remarkable he had ever spent with him.

Samuel was cheerful, even exhilarated. He talked about his life in a way he'd never done before.

Joel knew that adults were often odd, but it had never occurred to him that they could also be odd when they were going to die.

Samuel practised playing the drum every day. Morning and evening. And they spent hours poring over sea charts. Samuel told stories about all the ships he'd sailed in. And about all the ports he'd visited.

Joel did the shopping and the cooking. And the cleaning. He went to see Sara at the bar where she worked, and told her that nobody needed to go to help Samuel now that he was at home. She had tears in her eyes, but Joel hurried away before she started crying.

The only person he wanted to speak to was Gertrud.

But he didn't even go to visit her. It was as if he wanted to be in peace with Samuel.

After a few weeks Samuel became so ill that he had to go into hospital. Neither he nor Joel had expected it to go as quickly as this. Now Samuel was in a room with four beds. His pains came and went like breakers on a beach. They had taken the sea charts with them to the hospital, and continued their make-believe voyages.

They laughed often and a lot, sometimes so loudly that a nurse came to see what was going on.

But sometimes they were serious as well.

'You can ask Göransson to help you,' Samuel kept saying. 'When it comes to sorting out the flat and its contents.'

Göransson worked for the logging company. He was Samuel's boss. He sometimes came to visit Samuel in hospital. And Sara visited him as well. Even Ehnström came. Ehnström and his wife. But Joel always left the room when they were there. He hadn't forgotten what she'd said that time in the shop.

It was forbidden to consume strong drink in hospital, but Göransson had brought Samuel a bottle of cognac that he took a sip from now and then. It didn't worry Joel. He thought he would almost miss never again having to drag Samuel home when he was drunk.

Joel was alone in the house by the river. Every evening he left the hospital once Samuel had fallen asleep. It was still very cold. It sometimes seemed to Joel that the house was like a sailing ship with all its sails in tatters. Now it was going to be chopped up. Nothing would be left of it.

When he wasn't visiting Samuel, Joel wrote letters to various shipping lines. And all the time he tried to avoid thinking about what was going to happen.

One morning, while he was having breakfast, there was a knock on the door. It was Göransson. Joel offered him coffee. Göransson was a man who didn't beat about the bush.

'I'm sure you know your dad's going downhill. He's not got much longer to live. You're a sensible lad, and I've no doubt you are aware of the situation.'

Joel nodded. There was nothing he could say.

'I've promised Samuel that I'll help you. But first I have to know if you want to carry on living in this flat. I've spoken to the owner of the house, and you can stay on if you want to. For the same rent.'

Joel didn't answer.

But he had a question:

'Was Samuel a good lumberjack?'

Göransson looked at him in surprise.

'Yes,' he said. 'Of course he was. One of the very best.'

'That's all I wanted to know. And I'm not intending to stay on here.'

'What have you thought of doing with the furniture?'

'I don't want it.'

'You ought to think about if there's anything you'd like to keep. Then I'll help you to sell what's sellable: we'll have to throw away the rest.'

Göransson stayed for nearly an hour. Joel didn't really want to talk about all the things that were going to happen. But at the same time, he was grateful to Göransson for helping him.

When Göransson had left, Joel worked his way through the flat, picking out what he wanted to save.

The sea charts. The photographs of Samuel. And some old letters.

Samuel's discharge book. And the old alarm clock that had always stood by his bed.

But nothing else.

A few days later a letter arrived.

Joel was informed that he could sign on for a ship called the *Rio de Janeiro*. It was on its way from Argentina and was going to a shipyard in Gothenburg where it would undergo repairs. If Joel was interested, they wanted him to sign on at the beginning of March.

Joel was pleased. But he didn't know if he'd be able to.

Nevertheless, he wrote a reply. He spelled out the truth. He wanted to, but he didn't know if he'd be able to.

That same afternoon he told Samuel about the letter.

'That's a good shipping line,' Samuel said. 'And it sounds like a good boat. Good boats must have a good name. *Rio de Janeiro*. Names don't come any better than that. When do they want you to sign on?'

Joel tried to avoid answering. But Samuel persisted. He wanted to know.

'Of course they told you that. You can't fool me.'

'The beginning of March,' Joel mumbled.

Samuel lay for a while without speaking.

'The beginning of March,' he said eventually. 'And it's the beginning of February already.'

The last evening of Samuel's life, he'd got it into his head that he wanted to play cards. Joel had brought him a pack of cards. Samuel was in an unusually good mood, and wasn't in pain.

They played poker. For fantasy money.

Samuel bet a million. And Joel bet a million as well. But neither of them could work out who'd won.

In the end, a nurse came and told Joel it was time for him to go home.

'We'll continue tomorrow,' said Samuel. 'Then I'll win back all the money I've lost.'

'But you were the winner!'

'Well, we'll see if you can beat me next time, then.'

Joel was still sitting on the chair at the side of the bed.

'I used to play cards with Jenny,' Samuel said. 'And we used to have lots of fun. Believe you me. When things were good, they were very, very good. I've never regretted that she was the person who was your mother. It's important for you to know that.'

Joel stood up and put on his jacket.

'The cold isn't going to go away,' said Samuel. 'But it's warm in Brazil. There's no such place as the end of the world. But there is a place called Brazil.'

Samuel died during the night. After Joel had left he fell asleep and never woke up.

Joel was told when he arrived at the hospital the next day.

He started crying. But he didn't cry for long.

Instead he thought about the last words Samuel had spoken to him.

There's no such place as the end of the world. But there is a place called Brazil.

It seemed that there might be a secret message hidden in those words. That the end of the world is only a dream. A place that doesn't have a name. That doesn't exist on any map. But Brazil does. You can go there.

They asked Joel if he wanted to see his father.

But Joel said no.

He knew what Samuel looked like. He didn't need to see somebody who no longer existed.

Joel went home. Despite the cold he walked slowly. The first thing he did was to write a letter to the shipping line.

I'm coming.
Greetings,
Joel Gustafson

Then Sara turned up. And Göransson. And Ehnström. And some of Samuel's old workmates. Some old men that Samuel used to go out drinking with also came, but Sara threw them out without more ado.

Both Göransson and Sara suggested that Joel should go and stay with them. But Joel said no. He didn't want to.

That evening Joel crossed over the bridge on his way to Gertrud's house. She must have seen him coming. Or possibly heard him. As he went through the gate she came out to meet him.

'Samuel's dead,' said Joel.

'I know.'

Joel ought to have known that it wouldn't be news to her. Although Gertrud seldom went out, she knew about everything that happened.

They sat in her kitchen.

He found it difficult to look at her. If he did, he'd start crying. And he didn't want to do that.

They sat in silence. Joel knew nobody as easy to be silent with as Gertrud.

After a while Gertrud asked him to tell her what it was like, being a sailor. Joel told her.

She asked about Jenny.

He had no idea how Gertrud could have known that he'd found his long-lost mother.

Last of all she asked what he was going to do now.

'I've got a ship waiting for me in Gothenburg,' he said. 'Then I don't know.'

'You'll come back here, surely?'

'Why should I do that? When Samuel no longer exists?'

'I exist.'

Joel didn't answer. She was right. She was still there. And there were other people he knew and liked.

'You grew up here,' she said. 'All your memories are here. I'm sure you'll come back.'

It was long past midnight when Joel went home.

The house felt empty and spooky. Joel had closed the door of Samuel's room. What he'd have really liked to do was to lock it and throw away the key.

He went to bed. Thought about what Göransson had

said regarding the funeral. He wondered if he ought to phone or write to Jenny. But he didn't want to talk to her. So it would be a letter.

Joel sat up in bed.

He'd have to put a death notice in the local newspaper. He'd almost forgotten that.

But what should it say?

Samuel Gustafson
Much loved and missed

Those were not appropriate words. Not for Samuel.

Joel got up and went to sit at the kitchen table. He took out a piece of paper and a pencil. Thought about various possibilities. Then eventually made up his mind.

But when he went to the newspaper office the following day Mr Horn, the editor, frowned when he saw the text Joel wanted to insert.

Samuel Gustafson
Who has journeyed to the end of the world

'I don't know if we can print that,' he said.

'Why not? It's my dad who's dead.'

'The text isn't really appropriate.'

'Why not?'

'Mr Horn shook his head.

'I don't know if it's suitable.'

'But that's what Samuel thought death was. A journey to the end of the world.'

Mr Horn continued to shake his head.

'Have you spoken to the others about this?'

'What others?'

'The other mourners? The rest of the family?'

'There is nobody else. Only me.'

Mr Horn was starting to melt.

'I've never published anything like this before in the deaths' column. That's for sure.'

'But this is precisely what I want it to say.'

Mr Horn looked hard at Joel. Eyed him seriously for a long time. Then he nodded.

'I'll get a lot of flak,' he said. 'But if that's what you want, that's what you'll get.'

When Joel left, he thought that Samuel would have been pleased. He'd never had much time for God. But the end of the world was something else again.

Something that existed, and yet didn't exist.

That's the journey Samuel had undertaken.

The funeral took place a week later.

Joel was dreading it. But Sara and Göransson had been on hand for him all the time.

A few days before the funeral the local vicar, Boman, had asked Joel to come and see him.

Joel put on his best clothes and went to the vicarage. He'd never met Rev. Boman before. He was a new, young clergyman who'd only arrived in his new parish a couple of months ago.

Boman asked Joel to sit down, and expressed his condolences. Joel mumbled something inaudible in response.

'I saw the death notice in the newspaper,' Boman

said. 'And I understand that you were the one who wrote it. I must say the text was most unusual. *He's journeyed to the end of the world.*'

'Samuel was unusual,' said Joel. 'That's the way he wanted it.'

'How was he unusual?'

'He thought the house we lived in was a ship. And that our flat was the bridge. And he was a good lumberjack. Göransson says so.'

'An unusual man,' said Boman. 'Is that how you'd like me to describe him at the funeral?'

Joel could feel a lump in his throat. He was close to tears, but braced himself.

'Yes,' he said. 'Samuel was unusual.'

And that is what Boman said at the funeral.

There weren't many people in the church. Joel was in the front row, between Sara and Göransson. The coffin was brown. Joel avoided looking at it. He still couldn't grasp that Samuel was lying in there.

Samuel had gone away.
He'd gone on a journey.
He'd signed on for an invisible ship and was on his way to a port that didn't exist on any map.
But perhaps the name of the ship was Celestine?

Samuel's grave was by the west wall of the churchyard.

As the coffin was lowered into it, Joel couldn't stop himself bursting into tears. All the time he tried to cling fast to the idea that Samuel was on a ship on the way to somewhere. On the way to a warmer climate. But despite all his efforts, he couldn't help himself. Not at that moment.

Afterwards they had coffee at the Tourist Hotel.

Göransson told Joel that they would have to go through the contents of the flat the very next day. Now that Joel had decided not to stay there, other tenants would be moving in.

It took a week.

The furniture vanished. Joel packed his belongings in his sailor's kitbag and a suitcase.

In the end the only thing left was a mattress. A sheet, a pillow and a blanket. Joel would sleep in the house one final night. Then he would leave.

He said goodbye to Göransson and Sara.

And that last evening, he took a walk round the town.

It was still cold.

He wandered along the familiar streets. Paused outside the Community Centre and studied the film posters. Walked round the deserted schoolyard. Round and round until he ran out of strength.

He was in a hurry now. In a hurry to get away.

He went back to the empty flat and fell asleep almost immediately on the mattress.

The night outside was full of moonlight, the sky full of stars.

15

Joel woke up with a start.

When he opened his eyes it was completely dark. He felt freezing. It was as if the cold from the floor had forced its way through the mattress and all his clothes. He lay still in the darkness and listened. There was a creaking and tapping from the walls and the roof beams. He thought about all the times he'd woken up and heard those very same noises. They had always been there, ever since he'd been very young. So young that he had virtually no other memories.

He pulled the covers up to his chin and curled up. The alarm clock was standing on the floor next to him. The hands were lit up. A quarter to five. Half an hour from now the clock would ring.

He could feel a pain in his stomach. Something was stabbing at him. It was his very last night in the house by the river. His last night and his last morning. He was about to leave. New people would move in that very same day. They would bring with them different furniture, and hang different pictures on the walls. Then there would be no trace left of Samuel or Joel. Time would pass. Other voices would be heard in the two bedrooms and the kitchen. Other fingers would make marks on the wallpaper. Other ears would be woken up during the cold winter nights by the beams groaning and creaking inside the walls. Soon nobody would remember that a lumberjack and his son had once lived in this house.

That hurt. The idea was massive and scary. Joel curled up as tightly as he could.

He wished everything had been as before. That Samuel's snores would come rolling through the half-open door. But everything was silent. Apart from the walls groaning and creaking in the cold.

When he was little, he'd sometimes thought that it was possible to bring time to a standstill. To cling on to a moment he'd enjoyed. But that wasn't possible any longer. Joel wondered what exactly it meant, being grown up. Before, he'd have asked Samuel. But that wasn't possible any more.

Nothing would be like it used to be. Nothing at all.

I'm so lonely now, Joel thought.

Samuel is dead. And Jenny Rydén can never be my mum. She can only be a friend. In the same way that Eva and Maria can only be my friends.

In a few hours' time I shall leave this place.

Nobody will come to the station to wave me off. Nobody will notice that I vanish.

Joel could feel that he was starting to cry. He didn't want to do that. He was fifteen years old, and a sailor. Somebody like that doesn't cry. Children can cry. And adults. But not somebody who's fifteen years old. That's an age when it's forbidden to give in to anything. Especially tears.

Joel listened. The walls creaked. He allowed the thoughts and memories to wander through his mind. He'd always lived in this house. Once upon a time Mummy Jenny had lived here as well. But one morning she packed a suitcase and went away. He'd been so little at the time that he didn't remember it happening. The only person around for the whole of Joel's life had been Samuel. Nobody else. Samuel with his drooping shoulders and badly shaved cheeks, his tired eyes and his longing for the sea.

Celestine had always been there as well, in her case. And the sea charts over which they had made their fantasy voyages together.

Joel wondered if Samuel had ever really believed that he would go to sea again. Or had it only been an impossible dream? From the very start? Joel didn't know. And now it was too late to find an answer.

Everything that had existed before was now too late. Samuel was lying in the churchyard. He would never speak to anybody again. His voice was dead. Samuel with his badly shaved cheeks. And his drooping shoulders.

Joel made another attempt to understand. What exactly did it mean, being dead? How long would anybody have to be dead? A thousand years? Or longer? He thought the worst thing about it was having to be dead for such a long time. What existed before you were born didn't count. But afterwards, when your life was over, what existed then? Samuel hadn't merely gone out for a short walk. He was lying under the ground, and would be dead so long that nobody knew how long that would be. Or perhaps there was no end?

He noticed that the pain in his stomach was getting worse now. He got up and folded up the blanket. He felt very uneasy, but there was nothing he could do about that. It was a bit easier if he moved about. He wrapped the blanket round his shoulders. He went to the kitchen, then clambered up into the window seat. It was a cold night. The single streetlight lit up the snow-covered road. Everything was motionless. The only thing moving was invisible time passing. Somewhere out there in the darkness and the cold, a new morning was waiting.

Joel suddenly recalled that night when he'd been sitting on the window seat and seen a solitary dog walking away down the street. That was a lot of years ago. But he'd never managed to forget that dog. He started to think about it yet again. Where had it been heading for? For a whole year Joel had run a secret society whose only task was to look for that secretive dog. Then he hadn't thought about it for quite a long time.

But now it was as if the dog had returned.

He strained his eyes. He felt certain that the dog would come running out of the darkness on silent paws. From the opposite direction. To say goodbye. He could feel his heart starting to beat faster, But the road was deserted.

Joel stood up. The light from the streetlamp shone into the kitchen. He shuddered. Now all he wanted was to get away as quickly as possible. The empty flat scared him. The walls were no longer creaking. It seemed as if they were howling.

Perhaps a house was capable of grieving as well? Perhaps the walls were howling over the loss of Samuel? Samuel who was now lying under the ground and would never come trudging up those stairs again. Joel folded the blanket and quickly fastened his boots. He'd put the alarm clock on the kitchen table. He thought he could see the marks made on the wall by the case containing *Celestine*.

Then he found himself in two minds.

It was still far too soon to go to the station. But he didn't want to stay in the flat. He picked up his suitcase and his sailor's kitbag and walked down the stairs for the last time. He hesitated on the last step. How many times had he walked up and down these stairs? How many times had he run? He didn't know. But he could still remember how proud he'd been when he cleared the whole staircase in three enormous leaps.

Then he raised his foot. The last step. For the last time. There was no going back now. It was as if he were opening a new door, at the same time as the door to his childhood slowly closed, creaking all the way.

When he'd locked the front door he removed his mitten and pushed the key under the door.

It was cold. He pulled up his scarf to cover his mouth and nose. What should he do? Wander round the old streets one last time before heading for the station? He didn't know.

But as he passed through the gate and entered the street, he made up his mind.

He would go to the railway bridge. If there was one

place he ought to say farewell to, it was the bridge and the river.

He hurried down the street and turned off down the hill leading to the bridge. He was walking alongside the railway lines. There was an old, rickety platform where the milk churns used to stand. He hid his suitcase and kitbag behind it. Then he started running so as to keep warm.

He had the feeling that there were several boys running alongside him. A full gang, in fact. It was really himself at different ages. He felt that he was surrounded by what he used to be.

He paused when he came to the abutment. He was alone again now. His ghostly companions had left. The arch of the bridge loomed high over his head. He couldn't resist the temptation to place one hand on the freezing cold iron. The chill penetrated him immediately. He shuddered.

At that very moment it occurred to him that there was one person he ought to say goodbye to. Gertrud. Noseless Gertrud who lived in her strange house on the other side of the river. But something held him back. No doubt she was asleep in bed. Besides, he didn't want to say goodbye to her. It was as if he wanted to cling on to something. Something that linked him with this little town. Something that would give him an obligation to come back. Not just to plant a palm tree on Samuel's grave, but also to meet Gertrud and say goodbye properly.

To prevent his feet from getting too cold, he sprinted over the bridge. He didn't stop until he came to Gertrud's house.

The light was on in her kitchen. He stopped outside her gate. Remembered the time when he and Ture had hacked open a frozen anthill and then thrown the bits into her kitchen through the window. He slowly opened the gate and crept up to the window. The snow creaked under his boots. He raised himself on tiptoe.

The kitchen was empty. Gertrud sometimes left a light on when she went to bed. She was bound to be fast asleep now. He tiptoed further along the wall until he came to her bedroom window. When he pressed his cheek against the windowpane he could hear her snoring. But how could somebody without a nose snore? He regretted the thought.

He ought not to think like that about Gertrud.

Despite everything, she was one of the few friends he had.

He didn't know where the feeling came from.

But all of a sudden he had been transformed into the loneliest person in existence. He thought he could step outside himself and observe himself from a distance. In the middle of the night, in the freezing cold. A boy aged fifteen standing next to a window and listening to somebody snoring. He felt the urge to cry. He left the scene. Ran up the hill, over the bridge, and didn't stop until he got back to his case and his kitbag.

He was bending down to pick them up when he noticed tracks in the snow. They weren't his own. Something else had been there.

A dog.

He straightened up and looked round.

He tried to spot it in the cold moonlight. But there was no dog to be seen. He started to follow the tracks. They led down to the river. The snow was deep. He had to plough his way through it. But he knew now that the dog had returned. The dog that had once been heading for a distant star.

It had returned in order to say farewell.

He forced his way through the thick bushes on the bank of the river. The tracks led straight out onto the frozen river. He tried to spot the dog in the moonlight. He carefully made his way onto the snow-covered ice. The effort had made him sweaty. But there was no way he could turn back. Not now when he was so close.

The pawmarks in the snow were very clear. Before long he was a long way out onto the ice. The arch of the bridge loomed up like an enormous animal crouching by his side.

And then the tracks came to an end.

Joel looked round. He didn't understand what he could see. Absolutely clear pawmarks that suddenly petered out. There was no hole in the ice. Nothing but an expanse of white, virgin snow.

He looked up at the night sky and turned his back on the moon. There was only one possible explanation, he thought. An explanation that somebody who has reached the age of fifteen shouldn't really believe in. That the dog had taken off and flown away on invisible wings. Heading for the star he'd selected to be his goal.

I must be childish to believe that such a scenario is possible, Joel thought. Now, when my father's dead and I'm a sailor, I can't be childish any longer. Even if I am.

Joel turned and went back to the river bank. He paused once, turned round and gazed up at the sky.

The dog was somewhere up there, flapping its invisible wings.

Joel retrieved his suitcase and his kitbag and walked through the deserted little town. When he came to the station, he found that the waiting room was still locked. He put his bags behind a dustbin and walked out onto the tracks. Stood between the rails and gazed southwards. He was in a hurry now. Not long ago he'd have liked to put time on hold. Now it was passing far too slowly. He was in a hurry to get away.

Somebody eventually came and unlocked the waiting room. Joel went in and sat down. He could feel the warmth returning to his body. He checked his inside pocket, to make sure he had his rail ticket and his discharge book. And in his pocket was his money. Eighty kronor.

An old man with a rucksack came into the waiting room and sat down. He nodded a greeting to Joel.

'Off on a trip, are you?' he said.

Joel mumbled something inaudible in reply. He had no desire to talk to anybody just at the moment.

'I'm going to Orsa,' said the old man.

'I'm going further than that,' said Joel.

'Are you going to Mora?'

'I'm going to the end of the world,' said Joel.

The old man looked thoughtfully at him.

Joel stood up and examined the map hanging on the wall. He found Gothenburg. And the harbour. And the shipyard. And the ship that was waiting for him.

The train arrived. The engine snorted and sighed. Joel scanned the platform before boarding the train, but needless to say, there was nobody there to wave goodbye to him.

Only Samuel's ghost. Standing there nodding to him, and whispering:

'Off you go.'

As the train passed over the railway bridge Joel contemplated his reflection in the frozen windowpane.

He was on his way now. On his way at last. Away from the little town he'd grown up in. On his way to Pitcairn Island. To the end of the world.

That existed and yet didn't exist.

Three days later, shortly before dawn, the cargo ship *Rio de Janeiro* left Gothenburg. Joel woke up in his cabin when the engines started to throb.

It was late winter, 1960.

During the next few years Joel signed on with several different ships. At the beginning of 1963, a few days before his eighteenth birthday, he worked on a little cargo boat that docked at Pitcairn Island.

While on shore leave, he collected a coconut from a coconut palm.

At the beginning of December that same year, he

returned to Sweden and made the long trip back to the little town where he was born.

In the evening of December 4 he got off the train and made his way straight to the churchyard. He dug away the snow and planted the coconut in the frozen soil on Samuel's grave. He knew it wouldn't survive, so he also spread out a few palm leaves he'd brought with him from Pitcairn Island.

The following day Joel left the little town.

He'd spent the night in a boarding house.

He didn't pay a visit to Gertrud in her house on the other side of the river.

When his train left the station, there was nobody there to wave goodbye to him this time either.

His childhood was over.

Joel had begun his long journey out into the world.

And somewhere up there, over his head, there would always be an invisible dog flapping its invisible wings.

A Bridge
to the Stars

It's an icy night in Northern Sweden, and Joel, unable to sleep, is drawn outside to haunt the streets. He finds the night-time activity of his stolid town mesmerizing in its unexpectedness and variety. But can he deal with the knowledge that he gains about his neighbours, his father, and himself?

'This is a deep, serious story, written with the lightest of touches and no hint of condescension.'
GUARDIAN

Shadows in the Twilight

Joel thinks nothing's going on in his small
town. But he's wrong. One day, a miracle
happens to him. He's very nearly run over
by a bus, but is miraculously unhurt.
Shouldn't he show gratitude somehow?
Surely a good deed of some sort is in order.
But what?

'Mankell's story always hovers on the edge of
magical realism but he suggests that there is
no magic as powerful as the imagination of a
melancholy child.'
OBSERVER

'Translated beautifully by Laurie Thompson . . .
there is no need to have read the previous book to
be entranced by this one.'
TES

WHEN THE SNOW FELL

It was all to do with Otto's magazines.
Where more or less naked women were climbing
up ladders, or sitting on balconies . . . He couldn't
say whether what was happening inside him was
good or not. But it worried him. It was on fire.

Joel is growing up. He is getting interested in girls.
Just look at his New Year's resolutions: 1 – to see
a naked lady, 2 – to toughen himself up so that he
can live to be a hundred, and 3 – to see the sea.
They all look pretty impossible for a motherless
eleven year old in Northern Sweden. And then he
saves old Simon from death in the icy woods,
and Joel becomes a local hero.